CROSSING GRAY STREET

CROSSING GRAY STREET

CAROLYN CROOP

Copyright 2020 © Carolyn Croop.

All rights reserved. No part of this book may be reproduced in any form or by any electronic or mechanical means, including information storage and retrieval systems, without permission in writing from the publisher, except by reviewers, who may quote brief passages in a review.

ISBN: 978-1-956074-72-7 (Paperback Edition)
ISBN: 978-1-956074-73-4 (Hardcover Edition)
ISBN: 978-1-956074-71-0 (E-book Edition)

Some characters and events in this book are fictitious. Any similarity to real persons, living or dead, is coincidental and not intended by the author.

Book Ordering Information

Phone Number: 315 288-7939 ext. 1000 or 347-901-4920
Email: info@globalsummithouse.com
Global Summit House
www.globalsummithouse.com

Printed in the United States of America

DEDICATION

In loving memory of

My dad

FORWARD

I only have one thing to say to my readers. I hope you enjoy this book as much as I enjoyed writing it!

CONTENTS

Dedication v
Forward vii

Chapter 1 1
Chapter 2 3
Chapter 3 5
Chapter 4 8
Chapter 5 11
Chapter 6 13
Chapter 7 18
Chapter 8 20
Chapter 9 22
Chapter 10 24
Chapter 11 26
Chapter 12 29
Chapter 13 32
Chapter 14 36
Chapter 15 39
Chapter 16 41
Chapter 17 43
Chapter 18 46
Chapter 19 50
Chapter 20 53
Chapter 21 56
Chapter 22 58
Chapter 23 60
Chapter 24 62
Chapter 25 64

Chapter 26 66
Chapter 27 69
Chapter 28 71
Chapter 29 73
Chapter 30 77
Chapter 31 79
Chapter 32 82
Chapter 33 85
Chapter 34 88
Chapter 35 90
Chapter 36 92
Chapter 37 95
Chapter 38 98
Chapter 39 102
Chapter 40 106
Chapter 41 108
Chapter 42 110
Chapter 43 114
Chapter 44 117
Chapter 45 120
Chapter 46 122
Chapter 47 125
Chapter 48 128
Chapter 49 130
Chapter 50 132
Chapter 51 135
Chapter 52 138
Chapter 53 141
Chapter 54 143

Reference 145
   Ghosts to Angels Graduate Ceremony Brochure 145
   Giovanni's Corner Restaurant Vegetarian Dinner Menu 148

CHAPTER 1

My world could not have been any more perfect. I had recently moved in with the love of my life on Adalyn Drive. I never lacked anything, and I surrounded myself with neighbors who are kind and fun to be around. Although I sometimes wondered what it would have been like to have children, I didn't dwell on the thought. Matthew, my love, and I were in our fifties. We had known each other since we were teenagers. People told me that I appeared to be in my late thirties or early forties. Matthew and I were to never age beyond our fifties. We had bathed in the Fountain of Youth, which halted us from growing any older.

Matthew had two children before his divorce. Thus, I was almost a stepmother, although I had not yet met his kids. Matthew had not discussed marriage, although I believe it is what we had both desired. I held Matthew high on a pedestal, which made me too nervous about bring up the subject. I am a bit "old school" anyway and think it is the man's role to initiate the marriage conversation.

My name is Adalyn. I take a walk every morning on the sidewalks of my neighborhood. Right before I go home, I stop by the park across from my house. It is officially called the Leonard Calvin Deter Memorial Park. Leonard (Lenny) died in his thirties in 1978. It is now the year 2019, so that was a long time ago. Lenny was my best friend, but not in life. I did not get the privilege to know Lenny until after he died. We rode the ghost train to Heaven's Station together. I called Lenny my personal encyclopedia because he knew facts about everything. He was fun to be with and sometimes broke the rules and went beyond the limits.

I lost many years with the love of my life. I had moved on from the teenage years and went from relationship to relationship, never really finding love. Deep within my head and heart, I never forgot about Matthew. We reconnected years later. Matthew is now my lover and best friend. Leonard is resting in peace, as is my head and heart.

CHAPTER 2

I enjoyed Christmas so much that I was known to put the Christmas tree up on November first of each year. The year of 2019 was no exception. It was, however, the first Christmas at mine and Matthew's house. As well, it was our first Christmas together.

The warm crackling fireplace created a cozy feeling for us both. Matthew had set a card table up in front of the fireplace, complete with a candle and a rose. We spent hours in the kitchen preparing our Christmas dinner. Matthew occasionally gave me a hug as I helped cook the meal. I responded each time with a kiss.

Christmas day flew by quickly. Both Matthew and I spent much of the day receiving phone calls from family members. However, we had set aside the evening for ourselves.

By seven o'clock at night, our phones stopped ringing, and our meal was ready. I took it upon myself to play soft Christmas music as we ate. With the warm and romantic ambience, I thought that Matthew might propose. I had assumed it might occur after we were done with dinner.

After our meal was finished, Matthew began clearing off the table and taking the dishes to the kitchen sink. He said we could exchange gifts before dessert. I helped with the clean up in anticipation.

After the table had been cleared, we sat close to one another on the sofa. Matthew soon stood up and walked over to the Christmas tree. He picked up a rather large wrapped box near the tree and placed it by my feet. I wondered if it was a box within a box and that a smaller box with a diamond ring was inside. Unfortunately, that was not the case. Matthew had given me a karaoke set.

"It'll be lots of fun. We'll be able to sing to our favorite songs," said Matthew.
"Thank you," I replied.

I began to accept the fact that I was not being proposed to that night. I then thought that maybe he was waiting for my birthday to surprise me with a ring. I don't know why it mattered so much to me. After all, we lived together, just as though we were married. Nevertheless, being unmarried weighed on my mind.

It was then time for me to give my gift to Matthew. I handed him a decorative bag with a new wallet and tie. It wasn't much, but it was all I could do that year. He thanked me and said he loved the gifts.

I wasn't hungry for dessert, although I watched Matthew as he ate pumpkin pie. We both said we had a lovely Christmas with one another. It had been a treasured time together.

CHAPTER 3

Life knows how to throw curveballs at the wrong times. After spending a romantic and heart-warming Christmas with Matthew, we entered the pandemic in 2020. I spent two weeks in quarantine during the month of March. I did so because Matthew died four days after becoming ill and learning he had the deadly virus. My world felt dead too.

I barely had the strength to walk around the neighborhood as I once did. By April, I did get outdoors on a daily basis. I walked a short distance in the early mornings to sit on a bench at Leonard Calvin Deter Memorial Park. I cried alone at the loss of Matthew and talked out loud in agony to God.

"God, I love you, but how could you do this to me? I spent most of my life, never really finding love. Then I finally find Matthew, and I am the happiest I have ever been, and you go and take him from me! How could you, God. How could you when you know I've suffered enough?" I said.

I suddenly heard the voice of Lenny, saying, "God has His reasons."

As I looked up, wiping the tears from my face, I saw Lenny standing right in front of me.

"Lenny, is that really you?" I asked as I let out a sigh of relief.

"The one and only," replied Lenny.

"What are you doing here? I thought all of my ghosts were finally resting in peace," I said.

"Did you forget that I'm an angel now, Adalyn?" said Lenny.

"I know. Shouldn't you be in heaven?" I asked.

"How could I be there when I know my best friend is down here crying — in my memorial park, no less? I saw you from heaven's lookout tower. It hurt my heart more than breaking up with Melanie did," he said.

"You broke up with Matthew's guardian angel, Melanie? I thought you were considering asking her to marry you," I curiously spoke.

"That was my intention. Then Melanie informed me that she went to the Rebirth Application Offices in heaven. They're located on Floor 849. She was planning to leave heaven to be reborn as someone else," informed Lenny.

He went on to tell me that he was with Melanie the day she received a response. Her application had been declined. She became so furious that she met with God face to face. She had a tantrum right in front of Him and even hit and kicked Him. Lenny was in the midst of pulling Melanie away when she, all of a sudden, calmed down. She did so after God told Melanie she had won.

"God surrendered to Melanie?" I asked with a gasp as my eyes widened.

"That's right. He allowed her to be reborn," said Lenny.

"Wow, that's amazing," I exclaimed.

"Oh, there's more," he said.

Before continuing with the story, Lenny reiterated my prior experience with the devil. He first reminded me that the devil had been converted to a "good guy" and was adjusting well to his new home in heaven. I didn't really need to be reminded. Lenny and I had once been on a mission together to find hell, convert the devil, and bring him to heaven. Our plan was a success. The devil attended classes in forgiveness, friendliness, music, giving, and love before graduating into heaven. Thus, for a short period of time, the world was without a devil. Lenny told me my life was at an all-time high with Matthew due to the riddance of evil. Although, the world was off balance.

Lenny then resumed his story about Melanie. He said that God gave Melanie a new life, indeed. She had been reborn as the new devil! I assumed that the return of evil in the world was the reason for the pandemic, which led to Matthew's sudden death.

Lenny went on to say, "God believes in second chances. After all, He gave the first devil the chance to redeem himself. I don't know if He will ever give Melanie a second chance, though."

I was trying to wrap my head around everything Lenny had just told me when, out of the blue, he changed the subject.

"Hey, Angel. Come with me," he said as he reached his hand towards mine.

Lenny liked to call me "Angel" ever since we met. He said I was as sweet as one.

"Where are you taking me?" I asked.
"To find Matthew and dry up those tears of yours," said Lenny.

I took Lenny's hand as we walked for miles. We crossed Gray Street from the Greater Flower City side, where life is lived. The other side of Gray Street was for the dead, leading to the ghost train.

CHAPTER 4

As Lenny and I walked hand in hand, we came upon an old, run-down train station to board the ghost train. Ghosts travel the ghost train on their way to heaven. I wondered how I would ever be permitted to ride, being that I am alive. Lenny and I took a seat on a bench as we waited.

Suddenly in the distance, I heard the train's whistle. In no time at all, it was stopped right outside the station. The doors slid open, and no one left the train.

The conductor yelled, "All aboard."
"Come on, Angel," said Lenny, addressing me as he took my hand and led me on board.
"I need to see your tickets," said the conductor.

He was a new conductor and appeared to be thirty years old. Matthew had been the conductor of the ghost train previously. It was difficult not seeing him in that role.

I thought Lenny had everything planned out ahead of time. He did not have a ticket for me.

"No ticket, no ride," said the conductor without even a hint of a smile on his face.

All of a sudden, my guardian angel, Maurice, appeared. He handed the conductor some money and motioned him to be quiet. The conductor inconspicuously took the cash and waved Lenny, Maurice, and I to take a seat.

The three of us passed ten ghosts as we looked for a place to sit. Lenny and I chose a seat next to each other. Maurice sat directly behind me. He began a short conversation.

"Adalyn, why did you want to board this train, sweetie?" asked Maurice.
"Lenny is taking me to heaven to find Matthew. He died in March. I miss him so much," I responded.

Maurice looked at Lenny and spoke.

"And just how do you think Adalyn is going to get into heaven? Bribery doesn't work on God. I know firsthand because I tried it once. You see, there is this fine-looking woman in heaven who kept turning me down for a date. One day in God's presence, I handed him twenty dollars in return for a favor. I wanted the beautiful angel woman to give me a chance. God warned me that if I tried to manipulate Him one more time, He would send me to Floor 13," Maurice explained.

I interrupted to ask about Floor 13. Maurice explained that it was the floor of heaven for all insects. He went on to assure me that God would never follow through with His warning. Heaven is a beautiful place where fear does not exist. Lenny eventually answered Maurice's question of how I would enter into heaven.

"I know where the escape ladder is at Heaven's Station. All of the angels know it exists, but no one has ever used it. In fact, none of the angels even care to know where it is located," said Lenny.
"That's because they're in a better place," Maurice stated.
"Exactly. The escape route looks brand new because it has never been used. My plan is to enter heaven by climbing the ladder up to Floor 7. If Matthew made it to heaven, that's where he probably is," said Lenny.

"So, you're getting into heaven through the back door?" Maurice asked with a chuckle.

Lenny nodded.

"Well, I am not here to pass judgment even though you are crazy. I am simply here to protect Adalyn from harm." Maurice explained.

Just then, the train came to a dead halt. As I peered out the window, it was impossible not to see an endlessly tall building that read, "Heaven's Station." I had been there in the past, attending classes prior to entering heaven. As well, I had once been given an "All-Day Pass" into heaven. However, heaven is so vast that I only viewed a fraction of it.

The ten ghosts exited the train. Maurice, Lenny, and I followed closely behind. The only difference was that the ghosts entered the main lobby as the three of us walked to the back.

CHAPTER 5

Maurice, Lenny, and I came upon the escape ladder at Heaven's Station. We had walked a great distance to reach the back of the building. Heaven is so vast that I believe the escape ladder was actually on the side of the station. It would have taken years to walk to the back. However, I remained quiet about my assumption.

"Well, we made it here. There's only one way to go, and that's up," said Lenny.

Next, he began climbing up the ladder.

"Step on, Angel. Don't be afraid," said Lenny to me.

I grabbed a hold of the railing and pulled myself onto the ladder. By the time I reached the third step, I had noticed that Maurice was close behind.

"Don't look down. Keep your eyes on me and keep climbing," Lenny instructed.

The ladder ended at Floor 7, which was where we planned to look for Matthew. Being that this route was never used, the door leading inside was difficult to open. However, Lenny tugged it with all his might, and the door eventually opened.

Lenny entered first in order to case the scene. He was almost certain no one would know I was alive and not an angel. Many of the angels in heaven wore halos and wings, although it was not required. I was told it had been a fashion trend for thousands of years. Thus, Lenny assured me that my clothing wouldn't give me away. Though, he added that it might be a good idea to eventually ride the elevator to Floor 18. That is the location of the mall where there is a shop called "Halos and Wings."

After looking around, Lenny motioned me to join him. Maurice followed me inside. I had never seen that area of heaven. It was endlessly big and wide. I nearly lost my breath at the beauty it held.

"Come with me, Angel," Lenny said as he led the way.
"Where are we going?" I asked.
"To speak to God. He visits Floor 7 only on Saturdays to greet the new angels through the gates who have recently graduated into heaven. I am going to directly ask Him where Matthew is," informed Lenny.
"Um, Lenny. I have some bad news. Today is Wednesday, not Saturday," I said reluctantly.
"Check your calendar. She's right," said Maurice.

Lenny appeared a tad embarrassed, although he assured me that we would still find Matthew. In the meantime, Maurice said that I was in good hands and headed towards the elevator.

"Where are you going?" I asked.
"I thought I'd check out the casinos on Floor 76. I bet they miss me there. Pun intended," Maurice said, laughing at his own joke.

Maurice had a bit of gambling addiction. At times when I needed him, he was lost at the casinos. Thus, my guardian angel was only with me part-time.

CHAPTER 6

Heaven on the 7th floor was so enormous that I had my reservations of ever finding Matthew. I wasn't even positive he had yet graduated into heaven. What made my doubts even stronger was that heaven wasn't only on the 7th floor. It has endless floor levels. I addressed my concerns to Lenny.

"What if Matthew hasn't even finished classes that are a requirement before entering the gates of heaven?" I asked.

"Adalyn, I told you not to have fear. There's always a way. Remember I was a computer technician when I was alive? There is a floor for technology here. We're going to head up there, and I'm going to hack into the system. There's a list of each and every angel in heaven. We'll check to see if Matthew made it here. If he did, which I'm certain is so, we will continue our search. First, however, we need to visit the shopping mall on Floor 18 and buy you a halo and a set of wings," said Lenny.

"I thought regular clothing was okay to wear in heaven," I said.

"Oh yes, it's okay, but why take chances. I don't want anyone giving a second thought that you're not one of us even if I do consider you to be a sweet angel," Lenny said.

Lenny and I walked to the elevators. He pushed the "Up" button as we waited. After the doors opened and we stepped inside, there were so many buttons for each floor that I couldn't even see them all. Lenny told me to press the button for Floor 18, which I did. When we stepped out of the elevator, we were outdoors in a vast world of shopping malls. Trolleys drove up and down the streets of the malls carrying angel shoppers.

Lenny and I boarded a trolley and headed to "Halos and Wings." The clerk spent an hour with me as I tried on several different styles of halos and wings. In the meantime, Lenny sat in a chair, waiting for me to decide. I was almost certain I overheard Lenny say to himself that I was taking my time like a typical woman. I just let it go, though.

Once I made my choice, Lenny gladly paid the clerk. I knew beforehand that every angel had their own bank accounts and that God replenished their money whenever they asked Him to do so. However, I was uncertain about the work world in heaven. I had always imagined a jobless existence once you made it to heaven. I addressed the issue with Lenny.

"Who would ever want to work in heaven, especially when money is free?" I asked.

"Oh, that's easy. Some angels actually enjoy working. Instead of earning money, they earn privileges. As an example, working angels belong to a special club called "Club 777." Don't ask me any questions about what the club entails. I don't have answers since I haven't worked since I arrived in heaven," said Lenny.

I was stunned as we approached the doors to leave. Mia, an angel I had once met on the ghost train, had entered the shop. She greeted Lenny and me with hugs. It had been a long time since I last saw her. We talked briefly as she said she had to return to work soon. Mia had been a bartender when she was alive and continued to do so at the restaurants on Floor 24. After the food was mentioned, I started to become hungry. Lenny and I said our farewells to Mia, and we hopped back on a trolley as I wore my new halo and wings.

"Do you think we could get something to eat before going to the technology floor?" I asked Lenny.

"Of course. I'm not going to let you starve. Others up here eat just because they enjoy it. You, on the other hand, need to eat. Let's head up to Floor 24. I know the perfect restaurant. You'll love it, and there will be a surprise," said Lenny.

As Lenny and I rode the elevator up to the 24th floor, he handed me a brochure. The cover read, "Welcome to Heaven. Enjoy Your Stay."

"What's this?" I asked before opening the brochure.

"I picked it up near the gates of heaven while we were on Floor 7. I thought you might be interested in it. It lists all of the floor levels and their main purpose," he informed me.

When I opened the brochure, I read this list:

Elevator Floors

0B	Basement - Student Room & Board
01	Reservations
02	Forgiveness Training
03	Friendliness Training
04	Music Class
05	Giving Training
06	Love Training
07	Heaven's Gate
08	Concerts
09	Mailroom
10	Wishes Offices
11	God's Prayer Offices
12	Hall of Fame
13	Bugs
14	Dancing
15	Sports
16	Race Car Driving
17	Stargazing
18	Shopping Mall with Trolleys
19	Spring
20	Summer
21	Autumn
22	Winter
23	Rain

24	Restaurants
25	Movie Theaters
26	Playgrounds/Parks
27	Technology
28	Art Museums
29	Music Studios
30	Plays
31	Entrance to Lookout Tower
32	Neighborhoods
33	Libraries
35	Movie Studios
36	Art
37	Pet Grooming
38	Real Estate Office
39	Bank
40-69	More Neighborhoods
70	Domestic Animals
71	Wild Animal Jungle
72	Camping
73	Television Studios
74	Radio Studios
75	Fashion Design Workshops
76	Casinos
77	Card and Board Games
78	Beaches
79	Boating/Fishing/Water Sports
80	Sea Life Heaven
81	Prehistoric Creatures' Heaven
82	Dress Up Studios
83	Cooking
84	Parallel Universes
85	Gardens and Waterfalls
86	Hiking
87	Aviation
88	Worship and Retreats
89	Cities

90	Countrysides
91	Ski Slopes
92	Amusement Parks
93	Water Parks
94	Video Games
95	World of Make Believe
96	Chit Chat Rooms
97	Musical Instrument Studies
98-451	All Other Schools and Training Centers
452	Aliens' Heaven
453	Meditation and Yoga
454	Hair Salons/Spas/Barber Shops
455-776	More Neighborhoods
777	Club 777
778-848	More Neighborhoods
849	Rebirth Application Offices
850-998	More Neighborhoods
999-2 Below Infinity	A Floor for Every Year
1 Below Infinity	God's Penthouse

I was enthralled with the vast array of floors, though I had questions about a couple of them.

"God's penthouse?" I asked with curiosity and amazement.

"Yes. It's God's home. He spends every Sunday there resting up before the work week begins again. Monday through Friday, He spends on Floor 11 listening to prayers at His office. On Saturdays, as you know, He greets new graduates at the gates of heaven on Floor 7. He's a busy Man. He needs His alone time just like the rest of us," Lenny informed me.

"Interesting. So, what about the floors directly beneath His home? The brochure says there is a floor for every year. What does that entail?" I asked.

"You can relive any year of your life that you want. You can venture into the years you never lived through as well," said Lenny.

"Fascinating!" I exclaimed.

Lenny and I stepped out of the elevator and into a world of restaurants. I could hardly wait to eat.

CHAPTER 7

Lenny and I were on the 24th floor. We sat down at the "Corner Restaurant," which was close to the elevators. After placing our orders, Lenny asked to speak to the owner. The waitress said he would stop by our table shortly. Lenny told me it was time for my surprise. The owner of the restaurant was none other than Giovanni, a former ghost I had met on the ghost train. It was a pleasant surprise to see him as he approached to speak to us.

"Adalyn! Lenny! It's so good to see both of you," said Giovanni.

"The pleasure is ours," said Lenny.

Giovanni went on to say, "Adalyn darling, I see your time has come, and you're now an angel.

I didn't know how to respond without lying. Luckily, Lenny stepped in to speak.

"Giovanni, you know that she has always been an angel," Lenny said.

"Yes, yes, of course. She's a sweet woman. There had been rumors when we took classes together because she didn't look like the rest of us – you know, like a ghost. It's good that we took those classes, though, and learned not to judge," said Giovanni.

I changed the subject by saying, "Do you still own the restaurant on the first floor near the reservations counter?"

"No, Adalyn, I don't. I sold the business as the customer volume was low. I do much better here in heaven. This place cost a pretty penny, though. It's in a prime location, being near the elevators. If you're ever in the market for real estate, always remember these three words — location, location, location. It is the key to success," said Giovanni.

"Thank you. I'll keep that in mind," I replied.

Just then, I nudged Lenny and whispered to him to ask Giovanni if he has seen Matthew lately.

"Oh ah, Giovanni, before you leave, I have something to ask you," said Lenny.

"Yes, yes, of course. What is it, Lenny?" Giovanni asked.

"The conductor of the ghost train, Matthew—have you happened to see him here in heaven?" asked Lenny.

"I had always assumed he was alive. He never appeared to be a ghost, just like Adalyn. No, I have not seen him," said Giovanni.

"Okay, well, thank you for your time. We truly appreciate it," said Lenny on both our behalf.

Giovanni left to get back to business, and soon after, our food arrived. I had ordered eggs on toast with hash browns and orange juice since I missed eating breakfast at home that day. Lenny, on the other hand, had a fancy meal of shrimp scampi with a frozen daiquiri. It looked delicious. Lenny said it was so good that he asked to speak to the chef. We were both surprised to see Oliver at our table.

Oliver had been a ghost whom I met on board the ghost train. His occupation when he was alive was that of a cook. Out of the countless number of angels in heaven, it was ironic that Oliver worked in Giovanni's restaurant. It was a pleasant coincidence. However, Lenny took it as an opportunity to ask Oliver if he knew where Matthew was. Unfortunately, he did not even know that Matthew had died.

Lenny had taken two shots in the dark by asking both Giovanni and Oliver about Matthew. I grew uncertain we would ever locate Matthew. Lenny, however, kept the hope alive. He said that our next step was to hack the computer system.

CHAPTER 8

After riding the elevator to Floor 27, I was in awe at the surroundings. There were endless amounts of computers, arcade games, robots, phones, radios, and televisions, just to name a few. Lenny and I had stepped onto the technology floor. Suddenly, various angels were greeting Lenny with the utmost dignity and respect. It was clear that he was well-liked, especially on Floor 27. After all, computer technology was Lenny's area of expertise.

"Follow me, Angel," instructed Lenny as we walked over to a massive computer system.

I felt an enormous sense of pride being by his side. I had always valued our friendship, and I felt special even more so on the technology floor. Angels treated Lenny as though he owned the place.

At the computer, Lenny began typing codes into the system. I later asked him why he hadn't just used voice technology at the computer. He said that he was trying to be inconspicuous since he was hacking into the list of all angels in heaven. He really was a computer wiz because it didn't take long for him to get an answer. He informed me that Matthew was, indeed, in heaven. Thus, there was concrete proof that my time in heaven would not be wasted searching for Matthew.

"Where is your next brilliant idea taking us?" I asked Lenny.
"Stargazing —Floor 17," he replied.
"That doesn't seem very productive. I think there's a better chance of Matthew being somewhere else," I said.

Lenny had no response. Just then, an angel approached to ask Lenny for help.

"Excuse me, Mr. Deter. Could you spare a moment to help me with a technical problem I'm experiencing with Alberta the robot? Her left leg is malfunctioning, and no one can seem to figure out how to fix it," said the angel.

It was shocking to hear Lenny being addressed by his last name. I was even more shocked when he responded to the angel's request. Lenny said he had a higher priority and apologized to the angel that he had no time to help.

Lenny and I quickly walked to the elevators to go stargazing. He told me we had to move fast so that no one else would ask for help. I suggested that he take the time to fix the technical problem. Lenny enlightened me that being known as an expert in any field has one huge problem within itself. There is no break time. The expert is constantly in high demand. Lenny assured me that the angels would eventually work out the problem without him. In the meantime, we entered Floor 17.

CHAPTER 9

I wondered how it was possible to stargaze, being that Lenny and I were not on the top floor. I addressed the issue with Lenny. He explained that each floor is like a universe within itself.

"The components of heaven can be difficult to understand. Just keep in mind that with God, anything is possible," said Lenny.
"Oh, I always know that. After all, I'm alive in heaven," I said.
"Good point," he responded.

The nighttime sky sparkled with millions upon millions of stars. The ground was grassy with some hills to climb for a better view.

"Why are there no angels here? It's just us," I said.
Lenny responded, "Oh, I'm sure there are others here. They're most likely further down to the other end."
"The other end? I thought heaven was endless," I questioned.
"Oh, it is. 'End' was just a figure of speech," he said.
"Thank you for clearing that up. I don't mean to be nitpicking every word you use. I apologize. I am still trying to grasp the concept of endless heaven," I stated.
"Concept? An endless heaven is factual—not a concept. There, now we're even. I am sorry for nitpicking your words, too," Lenny said with a chuckle.
"Words? I think you meant 'word'," I pointed out as we both filled the open air with laughter.
"Look over there," said Lenny as he changed the subject.

He pointed to a display of telescopes mounted into a concrete section of the lawn.

"Come on, Angel. It's more fun to look at the stars on top of the hill," Lenny said as he led the way.

By the time we reached the top, I was exhausted. The hill was small, yet my day had already been full of adventure. I was ready for some sleep.

Lenny and I sat down on the grassy hill to stargaze.

"Pick the brightest star and make a wish," said Lenny with a tone of excitement.

I found my star and wished that I would reunite with Matthew. I then laid down and fell into a deep, restful sleep. It was the following morning when I awoke, yet the sky was still dark with stars.

CHAPTER 10

Our adventures led Lenny and I back down in the elevator to Floor 9, which is the mailroom nonetheless. I had never in my life seen so many rows of letters, packages, and postcards. When I asked Lenny why we ventured to the post offices, he said for faster service.

"What exactly do you mean?" I asked with confusion.

"Once you make a wish, it is magically placed inside an envelope and sent directly to the mailroom. We're here to find it and expedite its delivery to Floor 10. The tenth floor is where the Wishes Offices are located. Wishes are granted there," said Lenny.

"Magic in heaven? This is a holy place," I said, seeking clarification.

"Think back to your time in Music Training 101. Remember the magical flute? Mrs. Harper made it clear to all the ghostly students that magic exists everywhere. When you played the flute, four angels appeared. Their names were Nora, Olivia, Elliott, and Leon. Did you even realize that spells out 'Noel'?" Lenny asked me.

"How are you even aware of what occurred in my music class? You weren't there as you had previously failed Friendliness Training," I said, wanting an answer.

"Well, that's magic itself then, isn't it, Angel?" said Lenny.

We paused for a moment in thought. I continued speaking.

"Just because names spell out a word doesn't mean it's magic. Mrs. Harper probably had it prearranged," I insisted.

"I'm surprised with all your doubt that you even passed music class. Angel, you're making me begin to believe," said Lenny.

"Believe in what?" I asked.

"Believe that maybe some people simply will never believe in the magic of heaven until they die," he said with sorrow.

Lenny stopped talking and started to rummage through the massive amounts of envelopes. I wondered how we would ever locate my wish. Suddenly, Lenny picked up an envelope and waved it in his hand. He said he was certain it was my wish. The envelope displayed a large gold star on the front. Sure enough, when we peeked inside, my wish was inside.

"What do you think about magic in heaven now?" asked Lenny.

I had a slight smile with a look of embarrassment for not having faith in Lenny. We both had an unspoken certainty that I had been wrong. Lenny took no time to reseal the envelope. We rushed to the elevators. It was time to take my wish to Floor 10.

CHAPTER II

We arrived at the Wishes Offices. Lenny instructed me to remain silent as he approached the angel secretary.

"May I help you?" asked the secretary.
"I'm here to hand deliver this urgent wish," Lenny said, as he handed the envelope to the secretary.

Just then, the secretary placed the envelope at the bottom of a stack of envelopes. I almost laughed as Lenny immediately took the envelope and placed it at the top. The secretary sighed and rolled her eyes. It was even more humorous when Lenny tried flirting with the secretary in an effort to make my wish a priority.

"Could you tell me a little about this place? I've never been here before. By the way, has anyone told you today how beautiful you are?" asked Lenny.

The secretary ignored his second question and began to explain the procedure of a wish.

"Once a wish is made, it is sent to the mailroom where it is sorted. Urgent wishes are rushed here to the Wishes Offices. It was unnecessary to hand deliver your wish. Once the wish arrives here, it is sent to be further prioritized. If it is deemed your wish is crucially important, it is sent immediately to Floor 11 —God's Prayer Offices. After your wish has been prioritized, it is sent to our Believe Department. From there, all wishes are thrown into a hat and the "believe manager" picks three to be granted," explained the secretary.

I wondered what happens to the wishes that aren't chosen. I was yearning to ask although Lenny had instructed me not to say anything. He didn't want to blow my cover. Yet suddenly I found myself bursting out my question.

"What happens to wishes that are not picked from the hat?" I asked the secretary.

"They are sent back down to the mailroom where they are reprioritized. Most of them eventually arrive at the Wishes Offices again. Although, the entire process could take thirty years or so," she replied.

"Why does it take so long for most wishes to come true?" I went on to ask.

"Because prayers that are sent to the mailroom take priority over wishes. Prayers are rushed to God on Floor 11. Not all wishes are granted. There has been an ongoing investigation into it for centuries. The investigators have narrowed down the problem to be occurring in the mailroom. Some speculate that Sam, an old worn-down postal carrier, has been throwing away mail," said the angel secretary.

"Why doesn't he just quit working if he's too tired?" I asked.

"Because he probably doesn't want to let go of his Club 777 privileges. But as I said, it's all merely speculation at this point," she said.

"What about prayers? Do some get lost as well?" I asked.

"Prayers is a whole different department in God's Offices. There has never been one prayer that wasn't heard," said the secretary of the Wishes Offices.

"So, it makes more sense to pray than wish, correct?" I asked.

The secretary had a look of frustration. I think my question caused her stress. Just then, Lenny nudged me to stop talking. He later explained that the secretary and the entire operation she worked for would be unemployed if no one wished. Wishes are magical whereas prayers are more concrete.

I didn't know heaven could be so complicated. However, if the theory about Sam is correct, it would explain the reason for so many ungranted wishes. As complex as it all seemed, a lot was beginning to make perfect sense.

Lenny wasn't too mad at me after we left the Wishes Offices. He simply told me next time when he tells me to stay quiet, do so. Sometimes, I just can't help myself. I burst out and surprise myself even at times.

Our mission for my wish was completed. Though, our overall mission to find Matthew was still in gear.

"Where to now my friend," I asked Lenny.
"I don't know. I'm running out of ideas," he replied.
"How could you possibly run out of ideas in a place like this? How about we take the elevator to the beach for a little rest and relaxation? Maybe that will rejuvenate our brains to come up with a plan. If we're really lucky, maybe we'll even find Matthew at the beach," I suggested.

Lenny liked my idea. We stepped into the elevator and rode up to Floor 78. It was time for some fun in the sun.

CHAPTER 12

As the elevator doors slid open, I was nearly blinded by sunlight. Lenny and I stepped out onto a sandy beach beside a crystal blue ocean. There were hundreds of angels in my view though none whom I recognized. In a way, I was glad about that since I truly was in need of a vacation. The beauty of heaven is that you can do whatever you want, whenever you want. Every one of us here have gone through classes prior to entering heaven. Thus, we know the rules and know to abide by them. The angels had previously told me that some of the lessons they should have learned in life. Although, they ingrained in me that it's never too late to learn. This I believe to be true.

The sand beneath my feet felt warm after I removed my shoes. Lenny and I walked along the shoreline, picking up seashells. Lenny handed me one of his shells and told me to listen.

"Can you hear the ocean?" he asked.
"Yes. It's right there in front of us," I wisely said.
"I meant could you hear it inside the shell? You're always trying to be funny my friend," Lenny said with a smile.

I then noticed a long row of white shelves built near palm trees along the beach.

"What are those for?" I asked.
"They carry beach towels for anyone who needs them," Lenny replied.
"Heaven really does have everything, doesn't it?" I said.
"Everything you can imagine and more," he said.

Lenny and I took a couple of towels, laid them on the beach and sat down. It was relaxing just to watch the angels on the beach and in the water having fun for a few moments. Lenny then turned to me with a suggestion.

"Let's build a sand castle," he said with excitement.

I told Lenny that he had a good idea. The two of us used our bare hands to pat sand together to form a castle. I giggled and we smiled and laughed the entire day. I had never been so happy with the exception of my time with Matthew. Whenever I was in Matthew's presence, my heart felt lit up. His sudden death was shocking. I hadn't even recovered from the shock in order to begin mourning his loss.

After the castle was built, Lenny and I retreated to our beach towels. While sitting, watching the ocean waves and soaking up the sun, we brainstormed our plan. Our only idea was to venture to various floors searching for Matthew.

"What are some of Matthew's hobbies or interests?" Lenny asked.
"I hadn't even spent a full year with him before he died. We had known one another when he was fourteen, and I was fifteen. Our lives then led us down different paths. We didn't reunite until last year when he was fifty-five and I was fifty-six. He then died in March before his fifty-sixth birthday. In total, we had spent approximately six months of our lives together," I said to enlighten Lenny.
"Are you trying to say you didn't know him very well?" he asked.

My emotions began stirring inside. *I thought to myself, "Of course I knew Matthew well. He was the love of my life. We had so much fun during our short time together. We splashed around in the Fountain of Youth, we said our first 'I love you's' at a ski lodge, he bought me a car and he bought me a locket with the key to life."* My heart was filled with so much love for Matthew that I disregarded Lenny's question.

Suddenly I burst out a lie, saying, "He liked sports, boating, and aviation."

"Good. That gives us an indication of where he might be," said Lenny.

I then changed the subject.

"Can I take off my wings and halo yet? I don't know why anyone finds these attractive," I said.

"Adalyn, are you okay? Your demeanor changed suddenly from happy-go-lucky to angry and frustrated," he said.

Just then, I began to cry.

"What's wrong? You can tell me. We're best friends, remember?" Lenny stated.

"You called me Adalyn. What happened to calling me Angel?" I said as I continued sobbing.

"Awe, I'm sorry, Angel. I wasn't aware of how much that meant to you," he said as he wiped the tears from my eyes.

My guardian angel, Maurice, then appeared wearing a t-shirt, shorts, and sunglasses. He grabbed a beach towel and sat right beside us.

"Nice day, isn't it?" said Maurice as sighed to relax.
"What are you doing here?" asked Lenny.
"Soaking in some rays on this bright sunny day," he replied.
"At the same spot as us. I don't find that to be a coincidence," said Lenny.
You're right. Oh yes. I'm also here to check up on Adalyn. You know, I don't only protect her physical being, I guard her emotional being as well. What did you do to make her cry?" asked Maurice.

Lenny was a bit distraught. I stepped in and told Maurice that I had been crying over the loss of Matthew. He accepted my response but said he was planning to stick around us for a while. Maurice did just that. He ventured with Lenny and I as we rode the elevator in search of Matthew.

CHAPTER 13

Lenny decided to make a game out of searching for Matthew. Inside the elevator, he placed his hands over my eyes and told me to press a floor number. I wasn't tall enough to reach most of them. My finger randomly pushed a button and we jetted down to Floor 15. Before stepping outside the elevator, Lenny showed me that the button pad slides up and down in order to press higher numbers. I had never seen such a thing. He then said that next time it would be his turn, though. I thanked him for teaching me about the buttons as Maurice, Lenny, and I exited the elevator.

We walked about on Floor 15, which was the location for all different kinds of sports. I took our walk as an opportunity to talk to Maurice. I had a question that had been weighing on my mind for a long time. I asked Maurice to please explain why he had only been my guardian angel for some of my life. I had read that people are born with a guardian angel who remains with them throughout their entire life. Maurice explained in length.

He said, "At the beginning of the existence of guardian angels, God had intended for each one to guard a life for a person's lifespan. As centuries passed, guardian angels began breaking the unwritten rule. Some quit their guardian angel position mid-way through. That is exactly what happened to your original guardian angel. There became a shortage of guardian angels. Thus, I applied for the job and was hired to protect you on the spot."

"Why was there a guardian angel shortage?" I asked.

"It's a lifelong commitment. Some angels developed other interests. As an example, some met their soulmates in heaven and no longer wanted to dedicate all their time to being a guardian," explained Maurice.

"Couldn't that still happen?" I asked.

"Not anymore. Guardian angels are now required to take an oath. They must remain in their positions throughout a person's entire life. Thus, there is no need to worry, Adalyn. I will be your protector until your dying day," he said.

I thanked Maurice for clearing up my confusion. With great enthusiasm, Lenny interrupted and asked me what sports I liked to play.

"I'm fifty-seven years old. I liked volleyball, running, and soccer in my youth. Now it's no more than miniature golf and croquet," I replied.

"I was hoping for an answer of American football, baseball, or basketball. I wouldn't mind watching a few games with legendary players," said Lenny.

Suddenly, Lenny and Maurice were having their own conversation about their favorite sports teams. Lenny was an avid Miami Dolphins fan while Maurice liked the New England Patriots.

"Which is your favorite team, Adalyn?" Maurice asked.

I responded, "The Chicago Bears," even though I knew nothing about American football.

"Well, anyway this time here is dedicated to you, Angel. How about we play a game or two of miniature golf?" said Lenny.

I thought that the mission of finding Matthew had been forgotten. I know it seems sexist, but when sports are mentioned, men become narrow minded and don't appear to focus on anything else. They develop sports tunnel vision. My thoughts changed immediately when Lenny spoke.

"Maybe we'll find Matthew playing miniature golf," he said.

I guess the mission hadn't been forgotten. I was glad my thoughts were merely thoughts and that I hadn't made any controversial statements.

The three of us walked past sports stadiums, baseball fields, and swimming pools. Eventually we arrived at a miniature golf course located next to a soccer field. As I glared in the distance, I spotted Adrielle. I had met her on my first ghost train ride. It wasn't a surprise to see her playing soccer as it is her favorite sport.

I told Maurice and Lenny to wait while I went over to say hello to Adrielle. Yet, they followed me as they knew her too. After waving her in our direction, Adrielle stopped to greet us. I took a shot in the dark and asked her if she had happened to see Matthew. I didn't expect her to say she had!

"Where was he when you saw him?" I asked with bated breath.
"Inside the elevator. He said he was headed to Floor 23 where it always rains. It comforts him, he said. Matthew misses you immensely, Adalyn. He mentioned you. He said that the short amount of time he spent with you was the happiest months of his life. Maybe you can find him there," said Adrielle.

I thanked her about ten times for the information. I then told Maurice and Lenny to come along with me to Floor 23. They looked at each other in silence and then both looked at me like I was a crazy woman.

"What are you waiting for? Come on, let's go," I instructed them both.
"Um Adalyn sweetie, we have no problem going with you, but we kind of have plans to stay here a while. It just so happens we're here on the day of some playoff games. Those are very important games," said Maurice.

I was furious and spoke up.

"So, finding Matthew isn't important?" I shouted.
"It's important. What Maurice is trying to say is, well, we're going to catch a game or two first. Then we'll get right back to looking for Matthew," said Lenny.

Fury inside me erupted.

"How inconsiderate! Look, you two can gladly stay here. You were supposedly my best friend, Lenny. I'm out of here. I'll find him myself," I nearly screamed.

I began my journey back to the elevators by myself. When I turned back to look, the two were following me. The anger was still stirring inside.

"I don't want you to join me anymore. Enjoy your games," I sarcastically said.
"Let me tag along with you, Angel," Lenny begged.
"No. You showed me how much value our friendship is to you. Do not follow me. And my name is Adalyn," I said with fury.

I continued on. This time when I looked back, Lenny had stayed behind, but Maurice was still close by. I addressed him again.

"I thought I made myself clear. Do not follow me," I repeated.
"Sorry, sweetie. You can wipe bad friends from your life, but your guardian angel never leaves. Even if you want me to," said Maurice.
"I'll have to speak to God about that!" I ranted.
"Take a deep breath and calm down," he said.

Maurice was right. I needed to relax a bit. The two of us stepped into the elevator, leaving Lenny behind. I was momentarily satisfied with that, although I hoped I wouldn't regret my words.

CHAPTER 14

Being the smart woman that I am, I came up with a plan of how to lose Maurice off my trail—that is, if he didn't leave on his own. I would simply visit Floor 76 to gamble. Maurice would surely stay there as he has a gambling problem. It seemed a bit devious; however, I was confident that I'd have better luck on my own.

Maurice was being a gentleman and asked me what floor number I wanted.

"Floor 23, the rainy floor. I'm on my way to find my true love," I replied.

Maurice pressed the button, and the elevator rocketed to Floor 23. A light rain sprinkled down outside as the doors slid open. In the nearby distance stood a small convenience store. Maurice and I stepped in several puddles on our way to shelter at the store. Upon entering, we viewed hundreds of umbrellas for sale. It was a good thing Maurice was with me since I had no money. We both picked out a black umbrella, and Maurice paid the clerk. I thought I would ask the clerk if he had seen Matthew.

"Is there any chance you've seen a tall, handsome man come through your store lately?" I asked.

"That's a very vague description," replied the store clerk.

Maurice stepped in and said, "His name is Matthew. He's about 5 feet, 11 inches tall, dark hair with some gray. He's in his fifties."

"Oh, yes. I distinctly remember Matthew. He came through here about a week ago—chatty fella. I asked him what brought him here.

He went on and on about his woman and how extraordinary she is. He talked so highly of her that it made me wish I had found her in my life before he had. He looked kind of down, though. Is something wrong?" asked the store clerk.

"No, nothing to worry about. Thank you for the information. You have yourself a wonderful day," said Maurice.

Maurice and I left the store with our new umbrellas. We both were quick to open them up as the rain grew heavier. My wings were getting soaked, which made them more uncomfortable to wear. Maurice hadn't been wearing his wings.

"Is it really necessary for me to continue wearing the halo and wings? Half of the angels around here don't even wear them," I said as we walked side by side in the rain.

"It's not a bad safety measure to wear them. Besides, were you aware that the wings really work? You have the ability to fly, Adalyn," Maurice responded.

"I didn't know that," I replied.

"You've seen angels with wings flying around in heaven. You can do the same. In fact, if you're trying to fit in, it wouldn't be a bad idea," he suggested.

"I'll figure out the wings later. For now, let's head up that way towards the lights. It looks like there's lodging," I said.

As we approached, a sign read, "Vacancy." The area was surrounded with cabins. Maurice told me to follow him inside the main reservation office.

"You're supposed to be following me—not the other way around," I said with frustration.

"You are a feisty one. Listen, you can either dry off inside the office or stay out in the rain. It's your choice," said Maurice.

As much as I wanted to be independent and do things my way, I did prefer going inside. Although, I thought, *"I am not going to continue following and taking orders throughout my time in heaven. I think I'm going to go with my plan 'B' and lose Maurice at the casinos."*

After making our way inside the office, Maurice once again asked the clerk about Matthew. My timing in life has never been very good. The clerk informed us that Matthew had rented a cabin alone and recently checked out. I was absolutely clueless as to where he would have gone from there.

"Lead the way," Maurice said as we headed back towards the elevators in the pouring rain.

Maurice was happily surprised when I chose the floor of the casinos. It had come the time to lose him off my trail as well.

CHAPTER 15

It didn't take long for Maurice to make his way to the blackjack table and forget about me. I stayed inside the casino until I was confident that he wouldn't follow me out. Immediately after, I headed back to the elevators and pressed the "Up" button. As luck would have it, I was the only one inside the elevator. I randomly pressed a number and took no time to take off the halo and wings.

"I'm free!" I exclaimed out loud to myself.

The elevator doors opened to the breathtaking view of gardens and waterfalls. I left my halo and wings behind and walked into a paradise that looked like the Garden of Eden. There were about fifty angels walking and flying about the area. Beneath one of the waterfalls was a lagoon where some were swimming. There was even a rope tied to a tree that angels were used to jumping into the water.

Suddenly up ahead, I saw the back of an angel. I thought to myself, *"I think that's Matthew!"* My heart began beating faster as I approached him.

"Matthew?" I said.

The angel turned around, and my hopes died in an instant.

"Adalyn, it's so good to see you," said the angel.

The angel KC was standing in front of me. I knew KC from my first ride on the ghost train. He had been a florist in life.

Although I stood saddened, I managed to carry on a conversation. We reminisced about the classes we took together and our time on the ghost train. KC mentioned the new ghost train conductor. He said rumors were that no one liked the new one.

"Rumor has it that he walks around with a chip on his shoulder. I haven't heard one good comment about him. There isn't even a close comparison to Matthew," said KC.

Just then, tears formed and rolled down my face.

"Awe, what's wrong?" KC asked with concern.
"I'm having trouble locating Matthew. He died and entered the gates of heaven. I miss him terribly," I explained.
"Awe, I understand. I'm sorry. I'll keep an eye open for him," he said.

I wiped the tears from my face and thanked him. My hope was fading. It was Lenny who kept the hope alive for me. Though, I refused to regret not allowing him to join me on my journey.

From the gardens and waterfalls floor, I ventured to the floors for video games and movie theaters. I didn't run into anyone I knew on either floor. I couldn't even take time out to play a video game or watch a movie as I had no money. I grew hungry and wondered how I would be able to pay for food.

CHAPTER 16

Since I had no money, I rode the elevator to Floor 33—the floor of libraries. I thought that with any luck, Matthew would be there reading a book. I wandered into the first library I came to, which had three levels of books. There were buildings within the building of heaven. God was quite clever when he created the heaven. I wondered what more heaven entailed that I hadn't yet discovered.

I wasn't sure what I was going to do about eating. Luckily, I was only slightly hungry. In the meantime, I browsed the rows of books as I glanced at every angel to see if it might be Matthew. All of a sudden, I felt a tap on my shoulder. It was Ava, an angel I had met on the ghost train. Ava had a vast interest in science, so it was no surprise to see her at the library. We greeted one another and had a short conversation.

"What's new in your afterlife, Adalyn?" asked Ava.
"Matthew died, and I'm searching for him here in heaven," I replied.
"I'm sorry. If I see him, I'll let him know you're looking for him," she said.
"Thank you," I added.

Just then, the librarian approached to tell us to quiet down. When we looked at one another, we both realized we knew each other. The librarian was Hedy, another former ghost from my first ghost train ride. I informed her that Matthew had died as well. I then asked her about her husband, Alfred. She updated me that he temporarily left heaven to engineer the ghost train once again.

"I thought I recognized your voices," said an angel.

Evelyn, another angel from the ghost train, greeted us. It felt like a ghost train reunion. I couldn't stay any longer, however. I was growing more and more hungry.

"Would any of you care to join me at Giovanni's restaurant?" I asked with hopes that one of the angels would pay my way.

Unfortunately, none of the angels took me up on my offer. I traveled down the elevator to Floor 24 to eat. With any luck, Giovanni would allow me to begin a tab.

CHAPTER 17

The hostess at the "Corner Restaurant" sat me down at a picturesque window seat. I believe I was given a prime seating location because I told her I knew the owner. After the waitress took my order, Giovanni came out to greet me. I thought, *"The hostess must have told him someone he knows is here."*

"Hello, Adalyn. Where is your friend?" Giovanni asked.
"Oh, you mean Lenny? I don't know. I think he's caught up at the sports stadiums," I replied.
"Have you found Matthew?" he asked.
"No. I haven't had any luck. You haven't seen him, have you?" I asked.
"I'm sorry to say, no, I haven't. I'm keeping my eyes and ears open, though. Hey, did you hear the big news going around?" Giovanni asked.
"No, what big news?" I questioned.
"Rumor has it that there's a real live person walking around here. Not an angel. Not a ghost. A woman who is actually alive!" he informed me.
"Oh, wow, really? Oh um, Giovanni, would it be alright for me to begin a tab? I seemed to have misplaced my money," I said in an attempt to divert the topic away from the rumors about me.

Giovanni replied that it was unnecessary to start a tab. He told me my meal was "on the house." Luck was on my side that he paid for me. My meal arrived, and Giovanni went back to work.

My empty plates were taken away after I was finished eating, although I then ordered a cup of coffee. I had wanted extra time there to sit and think. I rehashed the events that occurred on the sports floor.

I had once attended a seminar on the subject of personalities. At that particular event, the presentation stated four different personality types. Every person's main trait fits one of the four categories. The remaining three can then overlap the dominant one to some degree.

At the seminar, experts tested me and concluded that my main personality trait makes decisions based on emotions. My second strongest trait is analytical. Therefore, I can sometimes be impulsive and later analyze my actions or decisions.

As I sat with my coffee staring out the window, I realized that I might have been overly emotional on the sports floor. I had been too harsh on Lenny. I had also been wrong in bringing Maurice to a casino. It was just as bad as handing a carton of cigarettes to someone who had recently quit smoking. I could feel my eyes beginning to fill up with tears. It was the cue to myself that it was time to leave.

When I walked out into the fresh open air, Lenny was standing right there! As I stood in front of him, I "broke the ice" and was the first to speak.

"How did you know I was here?" I asked.
"I figured you'd get hungry eventually," he replied.
"Look, Lenny. I've been doing some thinking, and I'm sorry. I overreacted. Will you accept my apology?" I asked.
"Of course, I will. I never lived long enough to form a strong friendship bond with anyone. I was too caught up with work. I was hoping to one day find a woman to share my heart. That never happened," Lenny said.
"Your time came too soon, Lenny. I'm sorry," I said.
"There is absolutely no need to feel sympathy for me. I am so happy here. I've got my eyes on a few lady angels, and well, can I still consider you my best friend?" he asked.
"I would be sad if you didn't," I replied.

We gave each other a hug at that moment.

"Hey, let's say we go find Matthew," Lenny said with great enthusiasm.

I was so glad everything was back to the way it had been. There is nothing like a loyal friend. I was more than happy to follow his lead.

CHAPTER 18

Lenny and I walked to the elevators once again. However, I was not prepared for what Lenny had planned—a ride to the top floor—God's penthouse!

The elevator rocketed up to one level below infinity. Even though we traveled at lightning speed, it was so far away that Lenny and I had time for a lengthy conversation. I began by asking about the purpose of our trip.

"Why are we visiting God's home? It's Sunday. Isn't that His day of rest?" I questioned.

"Yes. We're bending the rules a bit," Lenny replied.

"It seems unholy. I'm certain he won't be happy about it. And what about me? Once He sees that I'm in heaven, I'll be doomed," I said.

"No need to worry. I am going to approach Him directly face to face and ask about Matthew. In the meantime, you'll be hiding out," he said.

"Why didn't we just venture to Floor 11 – His Prayer Offices?" I asked.

"Do you realize the amount of prayers coming into His offices on a daily basis? He hears every single one. He is a perfect Man. He has never missed even one throughout the course of time. I don't want to interrupt Him during His work week and be the cause of His work getting behind. It's much better to talk to Him on His day off. Besides, aren't you curious about His penthouse?" Lenny asked.

I had high hopes that Lenny knew what he was doing. If God caught wind that I was in heaven before my time, there's no telling what my fate would be. Suddenly, the elevator jolted and came to a dead halt.

The doors opened at the entrance to God's home. The sign on His front door read, "Please knock."

"There. You see that? He wouldn't have a sign hanging up if He didn't want visitors. We're not going to be able to enter this way though since you can't be seen," said Lenny.

"Don't tell me we're going through the back door here too," I said.

"I don't even know if there is a back door. Come on, Angel. Let's check it out," he instructed.

As we began our journey around the perimeters of God's penthouse, Curious Lenny peeked inside a window.

"Coast is clear. He's asleep on the couch," Lenny said.

Lenny led me farther around God's home. It was much smaller than I ever imagined. I thought God would have the best of everything and be living like the king that He is. Instead, His house looked average yet, well maintained. Just then, Lenny began to slide open a window.

"Climb in," Lenny instructed.

I decided not to question anything else. I had to keep the faith that Lenny knew what he was doing and that everything would turn out fine. I crawled into God's home through the window and turned to help Lenny inside.

"Wow! This must be His art room," said Lenny in amazement.

The room was filled with painted globes, painted planets, wall murals of the world, paint cans and brushes, and an easel. On the ceiling was a window to the sky.

"I need to use the restroom. Do you think He has one?" I asked.

"I'm sure He does. God created us in His image," Lenny replied.

I found the restroom, yet upon my return, I heard voices coming from the art room. God had seemingly woken up from his nap and discovered Lenny in the room. I stood in the hallway and listened. The two were getting along like old friends.

"This is my beta room. I create worlds, stars, galaxies, and other odds and ends here with paint and clay," said God.
"How do you create people?" Lenny asked.
"With my hands, head, and heart. Now come to the living room. I'll show you my two fish," God replied.
"Pet fish?" Lenny asked.
"I don't like to refer to them as pets. They are simply goldfish made from my creation. Meet Cornelious and Bob," said God.

God seemed happy to have a visitor. He told Lenny to knock on the front door the next time. While the two carried on their conversation, I exited through the window to wait for Lenny. I was outside for an hour before I heard the front door open, and God and Lenny were saying their goodbyes. I couldn't believe what my ears heard next.

"Don't forget to give my regards to Adalyn as well. She's been waiting for you at the side of my house," said God right before he closed the door.
Lenny immediately gulped.

"Well, He is the 'All-Knowing God'," I reminded him.
"True. Very, very true," Lenny added.
"Okay, give me the scoop. What did He say about Matthew?" I frantically asked.
"Oh, He knows where Matthew is, too," said Lenny.

Just then, God reopened the front door to speak.

"Oh, Adalyn, would you mind coming inside. I actually do need to speak to you," God said.

My worst fear had come true. I was not going to get away with visiting heaven before my time. I then entered God's penthouse and sat down in a comfortable chair as He sat on the couch. I felt like I was at the principal's office only ten times worse.

As I looked around, I thought to myself, "God's house looks just like a bachelor's pad. He has shoes lying around, empty wine bottles, and He lives alone."

God began by saying, "You know for every action, there's a consequence, right?"

"Yes, God. I am truly sorry I broke in. It won't happen again," I assured Him.

"That is not the issue I am addressing. Where is it that you took Maurice?" asked God.

"I know, God. I took him to a casino. I was dead wrong to do so, being that he has a gambling addiction. I have realized my mistake. I am so sorry," I said.

"Well, the consequence is that Maurice lost more money that day. It seems he made promises to a loan shark—promises he couldn't keep. He is the first angel to escape heaven in all of time's existence. Maurice is at large with a loan shark on his trail." God informed me.

"But heaven is a better place. How could this be happening?" I asked.

"A better place, not a perfect place. I thought about making it perfect, but then I thought it might get too boring.

God was not out to punish me. However, He was allowing me to live with the consequences of what I had done. Not only was Maurice, my guardian angel, I also considered him to be a friend. As well, not only was Maurice at large, he was not around to protect me. Something had to be done, and God's plans were for me to work it out for myself.

I stayed to talk to God for an hour, just as Lenny had done. By the time our chat was over, I had realized first-hand how truly awesome He is—even more so than Matthew and even more so than Lenny. There actually is no comparison. God is His own unique entity.

CHAPTER 19

The elevator moved extremely slowly on the way down. It even jolted back and forth a few times. I hoped that I would be safe. After all, I no longer had a guardian angel watching over me. Although, Maurice did tell me once that he was always with me in spirit.

Lenny and I had a long ride down. I wasn't even certain of which floor number he pressed. Suddenly, the elevator stopped to let a lady angel on. She pressed Floor 454, which was the hair salons, barbershops, and spas. The lady angel kept staring at me and spoke to me.

"You look mighty suspicious," she said.

I stood in silence. I wasn't sure how to respond.

"You know, it's said there's a woman walking around heaven alive. Something about you seems off. You wouldn't happen to be that woman, would you?" the lady angel said as she continued to glare at me.
"No, it's not me. I hope they find her soon, though," I replied.

"Oh, God. I just sinned again by telling a lie," I thought to myself.

Just then, the elevator stopped to let her off on Floor 454. What a relief she was gone. After the doors shut, the elevator jet speeded downward before stopping at a dead halt. Lenny and I had been thrown to the floor. As I looked up, I noticed the buttons all blinking. I had no idea what floor we were on. Lenny asked me if I was okay. I told him I was just a little shaken up but that I was fine. He said he was okay, too, as he stood up to press the 'open' button. As the door slid open, I wondered which floor we were on.

Lenny and I stepped out into familiar territory as the elevator door shut behind us. We had landed on the basement level. I had been there before as it was where ghostly students spent the night. Room and board were located in the basement, the lobby and reservations were on the first floor, and classes were on Floors 2-6.

"We need to go up to heaven immediately. I have got to find Matthew," I frantically said as I took hold of Lenny's hand and led him towards the elevator.

I pressed the "Up" button and waited, but the door wouldn't open. After a while, I pressed it again. Lenny did too. I temporarily lost control and pressed the button over and over in a panic.

I began banging on the door and yelling, "Open up."

Lenny suggested we take the stairs. We looked at one another in shock. We both knew I wouldn't be able to get back into heaven by way of the stairs. The doors leading to heaven are locked at the sixth-floor level.

"Does this mean we use the back door again?" I asked Lenny.
"Apparently so. It's the only way," he replied.

Lenny and I took the stairs to the main lobby on the first floor, walked outside, and began our long journey to the escape ladder. We repeated our climb to Floor 7, only this time the door was locked. Not even Lenny, an angel from heaven, could get back inside.

"What do we do now?" I asked, still in a panic.
"I don't know," Lenny replied.
"You always have a backup plan for every plan. What do you mean you don't know?" I said.

"Unfortunately, I didn't plan for this. I've never been locked out of heaven before," he said.

"Don't you have keys?" I reminded him.

"Yes, but not the right ones," Lenny reluctantly said.

Lenny and I climbed back down and paused for a moment as we brainstormed our next move.

"You're not really stuck, Angel. Maybe it's time for you to return home," he suggested.

"I not only have Matthew to find. I have to search for Maurice too. Besides, if I went home, what would happen to you?" I asked.

Lenny didn't have an answer. I never knew him to be out of ideas. Our only course of action was to walk and hope for a brilliant plan.

CHAPTER 20

Desolate land surrounded the eternally tall structure of Heaven's Station. As dusk drew near, Lenny and I concluded it was best not to venture away from the building. We knew from experience that our journey by foot would lead us to the main entrance. Since there was nothing else close by, we thought our only option was to board the ghost train. Again, I wondered how I would be permitted to ride without a ticket.

By the time we arrived, the ghost train was stationed, letting ghostly passengers off. Ghosts that had failed their classes prior to entering heaven then boarded. It was standard practice for ghosts to reboard the train if they didn't pass a class. They were required to help someone before they could return to classes again.

"All Aboard," I repeatedly heard.

Lenny and I waited for all to board before we stepped on the train. I stopped dead in my tracks the moment I saw him. Matthew was conducting the train. We stood in silence, gazing into one another's eyes before he reached out his arms to hug me. We embraced without letting go for seemingly minutes.

Matthew whispered in my ear, "Oh, how I've missed you."

Suddenly Alfred, the engineer, interrupted. He was an angel without wings, just as Matthew.

"Adalyn, is that you? Hello Lenny," said Alfred.

Lenny and I greeted Alfred. We spent a few moments getting reacquainted. Matthew and Alfred were so caught up in the moment that Lenny and I were never asked for tickets. Matthew told us to find our seats and said he would come to talk to me soon after the train starts rolling.

Just as the engine started, a Man came out of Heaven's Station main doors, waving for the train to wait for Him. The next thing I knew, God had boarded. I think Matthew allowed Him to get away without a ticket also.

Onboard the train were fifteen ghosts, the angels Alfred, Matthew, and Lenny, and one living person —me. The ghosts all had bright white skin and white hair and wore their regular clothes. None of the three angels were wearing their wings. I didn't appear suspicious to the ghosts since I looked as angelic as the angels did. However, the three angels and God knew I was alive. Nonetheless, they didn't blow my cover.

God took a seat across the aisle from me. Lenny was sitting at the window seat next to me. I was curious about the reason for God riding the train, but I was hesitant to ask. *I then thought, "If you want a direct answer, ask a direct question.* I gathered my courage and began to talk to God.

"How are you today, God?" I asked.
"There is nothing to complain about. I couldn't be better. How are you, Adalyn," He replied.
"I couldn't be better either. Um, oh, I mean, I could be a better person. What I meant was I am so thrilled today because I found Matthew. Thank you, God. I'm certain it was because of you," I answered.
"You're welcome, although I hadn't planned for that to happen. That one kind of slipped by me," God said with a wink.

I knew God was the reason I was able to reunite with Matthew. I smiled back at Him as we both knew the truth. I then continued our conversation.

"What brings you on board the ghost train?" I asked.

"I never have had a vacation. I'm not one to follow the crowd, but I thought, everyone else is doing it, I will too. In the meantime, I have the angel Stella filling in for me. There is no need to be concerned. I trained her for two weeks, and I'm carrying my phone. I told her to call if she needs my help," He informed me.

"A woman is in charge right now?" I asked for confirmation.

"Yes. It's only her first day on the job, and she's already answered many prayers. By the way, I'm heading to New York City. I'd rather not vacation alone. I'd like it if you and Lenny were to join me," He said.

Lenny and I were not about to turn God down on His offer. We both agreed to vacation with Him. I asked God why He didn't choose a more relaxing location, such as Hawaii. He responded that He likes the hustle and bustle of cities because people are His favorite creation. I was beginning to wish I was in school, telling the class how I spent my summer vacation. No one would believe me.

CHAPTER 21

Matthew came down the aisle to spend a little more time with me. We couldn't stop talking and glaring into one another's eyes. We were so absorbed with each other that Lenny finally gave up his seat for Matthew.

"Where are you going?" I asked Lenny as he headed towards the front of the train.

"If God can get a temporary fill in, so can Matthew. I'm going to conduct the ghost train while you two enjoy each other's company for a while," said Lenny.

It was kind of Lenny to give up his seat. It gave Matthew and me a chance to hold hands while we talked. We said how much we loved and had missed one another. I told him I had cried every day since he died. He said he knew because he spent a great deal of time at the look-out tower in heaven. It was not my time to be sad anymore.

The train was rolling on its way to New York City. Matthew and I reminisced about the Christmas we spent together as well as our teenage years. In the meantime, God was preoccupied with texting on His phone. However, I think He was listening in on my conversation because He occasionally looked in my direction with a smile.

An hour before arriving in New York City, Matthew resumed his conductor role. Lenny returned to his seat next to me. I switched to the window seat so that God and Lenny could talk easier. It seemed God had some technical questions about His phone. Lenny had died in 1978 before mobile phones were popular. Even so, he was an expert with any type of technology.

The fifteen ghosts had exited the train at various locations along the way. By the time we stopped at Penn Station, God, Alfred, Matthew, Lenny, and I were the only ones on the train. Alfred and Matthew told God that the ghost train would be back in a week after His vacation was done. I gave Matthew a kiss before departing. I was going to miss him once again. Although this time, I knew we would reunite soon.

The ghost train had the capability to time travel. However, after glancing around at the numerous people at the station, I was quite certain we were still in the year 2020. Most everyone had a face mask on due to the pandemic.

God, Lenny, and I took an escalator up to the first floor of the station. From there, we walked to a ritzy Manhattan hotel located in Times Square. Along the way, God purchased food and a new outfit for me. As well, He bought the three of us face masks for protection from the deadly virus.

God took care of reservations at the hotel. He registered as "Mr. Jones." Each of the three of us had our own room. After catching up on much-needed sleep, God, Lenny, and I spent the following days touring the brilliant sights of the city.

CHAPTER 22

The morning began with breakfast at the first-floor restaurant of the hotel. Everyone who interacted with God showed Him the utmost respect. It was as though they knew He was God. However, they were unaware that He truly was the one and only Almighty. I suppose people treated Him with courtesy and admiration because of His charisma and confident demeanor.

Just before I ate, I turned to God and prayed out loud, thanking Him for my food. An obnoxious old lady passing by our table told me I was being disgraceful.

"Show some respect. Prayers should be said to God, not to the man who paid for your food," said the old lady.
"Ah um ah, yes, ma'am. I will be sure to do so next time," I said to appease her.

She seemed satisfied with my response and walked to her table. God then turned to me and instructed me to refer to Him as "Mr. Jones." I asked Him about His first name.

He simply said, "Jones, Godfrey Jones."

God, Lenny, and I discussed our plans for the day as we ate. There were so many attractions we wanted to visit during the course of the week. It was overwhelming to decide our first priorities. We especially wanted to see the Empire State Building, a Broadway play, the Statue of Liberty, Central Park, The National 9/11 Memorial and Museum, and the Metropolitan Museum of Art. We chose to begin by paying our respects at the memorial.

The tour of The National 9/11 Memorial and Museum was a somber experience. We viewed portraits of people who were lost on the planes, memorabilia of those who lost their lives, and crushed fire trucks. I cried as much as I had after Matthew died. God suggested we not stay any longer. Lenny agreed. From there, we walked down to the subway. I wasn't sure where we were headed. Thus, I was surprised to learn that God and Lenny were taking me dancing.

God was astonishingly a talented dancer. I asked Him how He ever found time to learn to dance. After all, He was a busy Man attending to prayers and greeting new angels entering heaven's gate. He explained that He is a professional multi-tasker. It was true that I had never visited the Prayer Offices on Floor 11. Though apparently, God dances each time He answers a prayer.

Lenny wasn't quite as gifted in dance. He stumbled several times, although he didn't give up trying. I wasn't much better. I repeated the same dance move again and again. I addressed both of our lack of talent to God.

"Are you having fun?" asked God.
Lenny and I replied, "Yes."
God said, "That's all that matters."

God, Lenny, and I were so caught up in dancing that the day soon turned to dusk. By then, we returned to the subway heading to our hotel. We then walked through the bright lights of Times Square. It was amazing to think my eventful day was only the first of an entire week.

CHAPTER 23

God, Lenny, and I arose early in order to watch the sun rise from the Empire State Building. The hotel concierge told us it was a magnificent sight. She said there was no better view than that of the "Big Apple" from the 86th-floor observation deck. I thought, *"Wait until she gets to heaven."*

Along our walk, God paid a ticket scalper for VIP passes to the celebrity green room of the state-building. Unfortunately, He was only able to get two tickets. Lenny said he would forgo the green room so that God and I could go.

I was quick to say, "There's a no bigger celebrity than God. He can easily get in for free."

Lenny agreed as God stood silent. Moments later, the three of us rode the elevator to observe the early dawn from up high. A tour guide then led us to the celebrity room. God handed the two tickets to the guide.

"Only two of you are permitted inside," said the tour guide.
"He's a big star," I said as I pointed to God.

Lenny nudged me as if to say not to blow God's cover.

The tour guide looked at me and said, "Oh, really? What's his name?"
"Jones, Godfrey Jones," I replied.

The tour guide repeated, "Only two of you are permitted inside."

God, Lenny, and I decided to go elsewhere. We shopped at a couple of department stores. God wanted to buy me more clothes to wear for the remainder of our vacation. He told Lenny and me that we were going to listen to music at Central Park that evening. When we arrived, worship songs were being played. As we stood listening, God turned to Lenny and me to speak.

"Gotta feed the ego somehow," said God as he winked at us.

Lenny and I were both aware that He was being humorous. I think God was enjoying His much-needed vacation. *Suddenly I began wondering about the angel Stella.* I decided to ask God if He had heard from her. He said He had been receiving daily updates.

"So, everything is going well?" I asked.
"Yes. Stella is working out just fine. So much so that I'm beginning to worry about job security," God replied with laughter.

Lenny and I laughed as well. Just before midnight, the three of us walked through the park heading to our hotel. I commented that it was risky to walk in Central Park at night. God reminded me I was in good hands. We returned safely to the hotel to rest up for the next day.

CHAPTER 24

As I entered my hotel room, I flipped on the light switch, but the room remained dark. I tried the lamps, and none of them worked either. Since Lenny was good with technology, I knocked on his room and asked for help. I was soon to realize that technology and electrical engineering are two entirely different fields. Lenny tried but he had no clue how to fix the issue.

God was walking by my room just as Lenny opened the door to leave. Lenny explained my problem to Him. Without hesitation, God entered my room and spoke.

God said, "Let there be hotel room light," and there was hotel room light.

I thanked God for His help and thanked Lenny for trying. Both then retreated to their own rooms. I was exhausted. Still, I had trouble sleeping. I usually read to fall asleep. Thus, I searched the room and came upon the Bible. I had never read it before as the number of pages overwhelmed me. I thought I would try to read part of the book that night. I learned that, apparently, God had turned dark to light before. I was then able to get to sleep as I felt comforted.

The following morning, God, Lenny, and I planned out the day during breakfast. We decided to make it a day of visiting the Metropolitan Museum of Art. Our plan was to then top the day off with an evening on Broadway.

God, Lenny and I began at the museum. The Metropolitan Museum of Art comprises three different locations – The Met Fifth Avenue, The Met Breuer, and The Met Cloisters. Two of the many famous paintings we viewed were "Self-Portrait with a Straw Hat" by Vincent van Gogh and "Bridge over a Pond of Water Lilies" by Claude Monet. We also viewed a collection of humanity's greatest accomplishments, encompassing 6,000 years around the globe. The visit to the museum took the entire day, as I prefer to take my time viewing artwork.

In the evening, God, Lenny, and I watched a Broadway play. I enjoyed the walk from the hotel to the Broadway Theater just as much as the play. The darkened skyline shined from the brightness of the city. Racing energy and neon lights covered Times Square. The sparkling city is unparalleled.

Everywhere we traveled, God interacted with people ranging from street vendors to well-dressed executives. He spent hours talking with homeless men and women, inspiring them with hope. His passion warmed my heart.

CHAPTER 25

The following morning, God, Lenny, and I made our daily routine plans over breakfast. Surprisingly, we decided to stay at the hotel to relax for the day. God and Lenny spent time at the pool while I caught up on sleep.

The three of us were prepared to tour the Statue of Liberty the next day. Suddenly, God was alerted with an emergency text from Stella. He immediately called her. Apparently, the angel, Murray, in charge of Club 777, was only permitting membership to his friends. Murray took advantage of Stella, knowing she wouldn't be able to do anything about the situation. All the workers belonging to the club were being turned away. Thus, they went on strike.

I was growing more curious about Club 777. While God was busy on the phone, I asked Lenny about the club.

"I know membership into Club 777 is only for those angels who choose to work in heaven. What's so special about the club?" I asked.
"It's a secret. I'll give you one hint. The word is "magic," he said.
"Can't you tell me more than that? I asked.
"Sorry, Angel. I've already said too much," Lenny replied.

God was done with His phone call. He had instructed Stella to remain calm until He was able to return. He then made a call to Matthew, demanding that the ghost train returns to New York City instantly. God, Lenny, and I hurried back to Penn Station. The ghost train was there waiting for our arrival. Matthew later informed me that the train traveled several hours back in time in order to rush back. Our vacation was over, yet I was in Matthew's arms once again.

Alfred got the train back to Heaven's Station in no time. Before speeding out the door, God spoke to Lenny.

"You can't stay here any longer. Come with me. It's time for you to return to heaven," He said.

Lenny knew better than to argue with God. He said goodbye to Alfred, Matthew, and me as he followed God out of the train. I thought, *"I am going to miss him,"* as a tear fell from my eye.

CHAPTER 26

I was blessed to have had God by my side in New York City. However, since He returned to heaven, I had a stronger need for my guardian angel. Alfred and Matthew both agreed to divert the train in an effort to locate Maurice.

"We'll try finding him in Las Vegas first," said Alfred.
"He wouldn't go there. It's too obvious. Besides, if he is hiding out near a casino, he would more likely be in Atlantic City. He spent some of his youth there, and he probably still has family there," I said.
"Where would he go besides a casino?" Alfred asked.
"I have no idea," I replied.
"Well, then I'm taking a gamble he's at the casinos," Alfred joked.
"Alfred, this is really no time for joking," I said.
"Since we have no leads and we know Maurice is a gambler, I say we look for him in Atlantic City. Let's get this train rolling," said Matthew.

Alfred went back to engineer the train heading to Atlantic City. Matthew continued his role as the conductor, and I took a seat behind three ghostly passengers. I decided to introduce myself to the ghosts since we had a long ride ahead of us. Their names were Della, Katrina, and Peggy. We got along just as though we were long lost, friends. As Alfred and Matthew attended to their jobs, the ghost train had an all-girls party. We talked about the latest fashions, shopping, and men. Della even broke out a bottle of champagne.

I explained to the ghosts that I was on a search for my guardian angel, Maurice. They all had their own theories on his whereabouts. Della was certain Maurice was at a church repenting for his life of sins.

Katrina's thoughts were that he was at a sporting event, and Peggy assumed he went to his former home.

Della insisted that I was better off without Maurice.

"Be strong. Be independent. You don't need a man to protect you," said Della.

"Don't listen to her. She's just bitter because she's been scorned by men before," said Peggy.

In the midst of our conversation, the train came to a halt. I looked out my window to see a sign saying, "Welcome to Atlantic City." I was surprised the ghosts hadn't gotten off the train anywhere along the way. They explained that they had grown fond of me and wanted to help in my search.

Alfred remained with the train while the rest of us visited the casinos. The angels and I were the only ones who were visible. I hadn't expected that Della was well versed in blackjack, poker, and baccarat. She was a bit bossy and advised me to participate in a game of blackjack. I wasn't sure how that would help with my mission, yet Della was highly insistent. I was reluctant to gamble. Even so, I played a few rounds.

Before my game of blackjack, the ghosts Katrina and Peggy were up to mischief. They rattled one of the slot machines. The crowd backed away in disbelief. Someone shouted out that the machine was possessed. Suddenly, hundreds of coins poured out onto the floor. Della nudged me to gather the money. I did so, as did the crowd. Thus, I had gambling money.

I had no idea what to do at the blackjack table. However, Della instructed me, step by step. I won each round. Matthew was watching close by. He told me that I needed to blend in with the crowd. He said my winning streak stood out too much. It was necessary for me to be inconspicuous.

I asked Matthew when we would begin searching for Maurice. He replied that I needed to lose my ghostly friends. He said they were a bad influence on me. Matthew and I waited for a moment when the ghosts were distracted, and we ran out of the casino. I wondered later if the casino was left to be haunted or if the ghosts moved on.

Matthew and I walked about Atlantic City in search of Maurice. It was like trying to find a needle in a haystack. The thought of quitting never entered my mind.

CHAPTER 27

It nearly seemed hopeless. Matthew and I didn't even have any leads. Maurice could be anywhere. Though, I wasn't about to voice my concerns with Matthew. I did not want him to put a halt to the search.

Matthew suggested we rent a small boat and ride along the beaches seeking my guardian angel. I think he had another reason for the boat as well. Matthew stopped the boat in order for us to enjoy a meal with wine. He even had one red rose inside the picnic basket with the food and drinks. I became so absorbed at the moment that I temporarily forgot about our mission. I mentioned it later, and Matthew assured me that he was continually watching for Maurice.

I believe Matthew knew our chances of finding Maurice were slim to none. I think Matthew just wanted to spend as much time with me as he could. I wasn't prepared for what was next.

Matthew was observant as he noticed I wasn't wearing the necklace he bought me when we visited California. It was a key inside a locket engraved, "key to life." I explained that the day I arrived in heaven was unplanned. I had left the house in the morning to grieve of losing him at the memorial park. I hadn't fully prepared for the day yet. Matthew understood. However, he suggested that possibly I was having trouble enjoying life without the key to life.

I didn't think I was having difficulty enjoying life. After all, I found Matthew, and we were together. As well, I was able to view the sights of heaven. Life was good. Yet, Matthew said it was time for me to go home.

"You can't stay here any longer. You need to be living life at home," Matthew insisted.

"I'm happy here, though. At home, I was grieving and missing you. You want me to be happy, don't you?" I asked.

"Of course, I do. Your happiness is my biggest concern. Listen, Adalyn, you know I'm in a better place. Look what I get to do —I get to be the conductor of the ghost train. I'll bet you didn't know that I collected toy trains when I was a boy. I even built my own train track. I had always dreamed of this. Don't worry, sweetheart. Your grieving days will ease, and you'll find happiness in life again. But you've got to give it a shot. Try sweetheart —for me," said Matthew with genuine sincerity.

"What about Maurice? He could be in danger," I exclaimed.

"He'll be okay. Do you forget that he's your guardian angel? You're not his guardian angel. You need to let go, Adalyn. Begin making you a first priority," said Matthew.

Reluctant to go, I followed Matthew's wishes. Alfred started the engine and the train rumbled on its way to New York. I was heading home.

CHAPTER 28

It couldn't have been more apropos that it was raining as the train rolled into the New York station. It was time to say goodbye. Matthew had a look on his face that I had never seen before. He stood tall and tried to hide his sorrow, though his eyes gave him away. He was going to miss me as much as I would be missing him.

Matthew handed me an umbrella and led me out of the train, where we departed with a kiss. I took a few steps towards Gray Street and turned back to watch him reboard the train. The door shut behind him, and the ghost train readily disappeared from my sight.

I crossed Gray Street with only an umbrella, my house key, and enough money to ride the Flower City Express. The train took me back to the world of the living. I had lost count of the number of days I was gone. Though apparently it had been long enough for someone to break into my house.

It was only a matter of minutes after entering my home that I noticed missing items. I was baffled that none of my valuables were gone. As I wandered from room to room, it became evident that only Matthew's nickel-and-dime belongings had been taken. I decided not to report the incident to the authorities as I had my suspicions. I knew that Matthew had given a house key to his daughter, Maddy, in the event we were locked out. My fury grew when I noticed my necklace was missing as well. The following day, I called to confront his daughter.

I was in a state of disbelief when Maddy admitted to taking her father's belongings without reservation. As she spoke about the sentimental value of each item, I grew empathetic. I took the focus away from myself and realized she was in deep pain. However, as much as I had sympathy for her loss, it did not excuse the fact that Maddy had taken my necklace. When I asked her to return it to me, she was adamant that she had never even seen it. I decided not to give her the benefit of the doubt. I was certain Maddy had my necklace. Though, I put the matter to rest.

I continued with my day going grocery shopping and doing household chores. Each day blended into the next. The emotional support and sympathies I received when Matthew died faded soon after. Maybe Matthew had been right. I wasn't able to enjoy living without the key to life.

As I unloaded groceries from my car to head inside, I stopped dead in my tracks. Standing in my path was Maurice. It was so shocking that I dropped my bags of groceries. He remained motionless with a face of immense concern.

CHAPTER 29

I was ecstatic to see Maurice, yet at the same time, I knew something was amiss. After gathering the bags that had fallen, I politely invited him inside. As Maurice took a seat on the couch, he let out a sigh of relief. He had been on the run for countless weeks.

I pulled up a chair to talk. I began by asking Maurice where he had been. To my surprise, he had, indeed, ventured to various casinos. Alfred and Matthew were right. In fact, it turned out that we had missed him in Atlantic City by a matter of days. Maurice went on to say that the loan shark was close on his trail. However, he thought he lost the loan shark when he arrived in Flower City.

"I think I'm safe—at least for a while," said Maurice.
"That's good to know," I said.
"I need to come up with a plan fast, though. I don't want to scare you, but this is a place that, no doubt, will be searched. It will be obvious to the loan shark that I'm here with the person I guard," he said.

I paused for a moment to think.

"What if you were hiding somewhere so evident that the loan shark didn't search as it was too obvious?" I asked.
"Where do you have in mind?" Maurice questioned.
"The haunted house on the end of Gray Street," I said.
"By my tombstone?" he asked.
"Yes. It's too obvious. The loan shark won't even waste his time trying to hunt you down there," I said.

Maurice liked my plan and my logic. The two of us took no time to get into my car and head down Gray Street. I parked my car at the old run-down train station located on the opposite side of Flower City Station. From there, Maurice and I walked to the haunted house.

Maurice and I stepped onto the creaky old front porch and entered the house. Only sunlight from the cloudy windows lit the darkened rooms. I hadn't been inside since I was fifteen though nothing had changed. Dusty slipcovers were draped on the sofa and chairs. The air was musty and stale. Daunting cobwebs manifested every corner of each room. I apologized to Maurice for hiding him out in a creepy, lifeless house by himself.

"Alone? By myself? Where will you be?" Maurice asked.
"You didn't expect me to stay, did you?" I responded.

Our conversation was interrupted by shaky floorboards and rattling furniture. Maurice thought it was an earthquake. Though, I explained that there wasn't a nearby fault line.

"Please stay here with me, Adalyn. I've been alone on the run for several weeks now. I could use the company," said Maurice.
"I think this place really is haunted," I remarked.
Suddenly, the voice of a girl said, "Get out of my house."
"I'm not scared of you," I shouted.

My response must have surprised her because, all of a sudden, she appeared by the graveyard window. She looked just as ghostly as the passengers on board the ghost train. She had white skin, white hair, and wore a raggedy white dress.

"Hello. I'm Adalyn, and this is Maurice. What's your name?" I asked without hesitation.

The ghost spent a moment in silence as she seemed taken back by my fearless introduction. In the next instant, she spoke.

"Emma," said the ghost.
"It's nice to meet you, Emma," I responded.

Maurice and I pulled the slipcovers off the sofa and chairs, and the three of us sat down. We spent the next hour getting to know one another. I began to cultivate a mellow ambiance.

I said, "I live in the suburbs of Flower City in a house that my soulmate bought. He died and is an angel now. His name is Matthew. We met when we were teenagers. In fact, we ventured inside this house together back then."

I wasn't expecting Emma to dig further into my life. She asked me how I spend my time and what I do for fun. I immediately diverted the focus towards Maurice to avoid answering. My response would have been dispiriting and heartbreaking. My life was sorrowful and lonely. I made a limited impact on others, as most people from my past had no memories of me.

"It's your turn, Maurice," I wittingly exclaimed.

Maurice proudly explained that he was my guardian angel from heaven. It seemed as though he was bragging. I think Maurice felt a sense of accomplishment and reward from his appointed position.

He went on to say that he was a casino owner in life.

"I caught the gambling fever at an early age when I lived in Atlantic City. It was the only place I had established strong friendships. My family moved from place to place in my youth. I was forced to leave my friends behind," said Maurice.

Emma was bold and asked Maurice about his love life.

"Since experiencing an unstable upbringing, I never attached myself to anyone after Atlantic City," he replied.

I knew Maurice moved around a lot. However, I was unaware of the degree to which it affected him until that moment. Emma was a bit boisterous and cut Maurice off from talking any further. She was inordinately anxious for the spotlight to shine on her background description.

"My life was extraordinary. I had friends and horses and a loving family. I even traveled to Europe twice. There was rarely a sad moment. My world was bright and sunny," Emma recalled.

I followed Emma's lead, and boldly commented.

"And now you're a ghost," I stated.

Emma gave a slight nod.

I went on to ask, "Why haven't you moved on?"

Emma had a look of confusion from my question. As our conversation continued, I grew enlightened that Emma was oblivious to her capabilities. It became obvious that she was lost in between the worlds of the living and the afterlife. Maurice and I spent the next hour telling her about the ghost train and Heaven's Station.

The day shifted to night as we continued our talk. I wasn't about to make the journey home on my own. I thought I would have to spend the night at the haunted house. Although, after I explained Maurice's situation, Emma enlightened me with some alarming news. The loan shark had been there earlier that day. It became pertinent to take Maurice elsewhere. I suggested the three of us board the ghost train and head to Heaven's Station. We immediately left.

CHAPTER 30

I never once worried about Matthew's reaction to my return to the ghost train. I thought there was no doubt that he would understand. After all, I was not only helping Maurice. I was aiding a girl at transitioning from a ghost into an angel as well. I thought that Matthew might even consider me to be like a hero. I was dead wrong.

After walking on Gray Street to the station, Maurice, Emma, and I waited only minutes for the ghost train to arrive. I heard Matthew shouting for all to board. None of us had tickets. Thus, I told Maurice and Emma to let me board first. I was certain I could convince Matthew to allow us onto the train. Indeed, he motioned Maurice and Emma to take their seats. However, he showed frustration at my return.

Matthew asked for the reason I wasn't home living life, as we had previously agreed. I explained my heroism in great length. After he listened to my entire spiel, he said I was not permitted onboard. I stepped off the train as the door shut behind me. I stood alone, staring at the train with sorrow. Tears rolled down my face when suddenly the door reopened. Matthew directed me on board and told me to take a seat.

I took the time on the ride as an opportunity to gain a better understanding of Maurice's situation. Additionally, I sought to brief Emma on the required classes prior to entering the gates of heaven. I began by talking to Maurice.

"Why is the loan shark adamant on tracking you down? How much money did you take from him?" I questioned.

Maurice replied, "It's not exactly about money."

"Oh, no. What is it, Maurice?" I asked as my eyes widened.

"It seems I got friendly with the wrong woman. I didn't do anything more than flirt. However, it turned out she was his wife," he explained.

I raised my voice and said, "Maurice, haven't you learned? You failed music class for flirting with the married music teacher."

Maurice replied that I was correct and that he knew the music teacher had a husband. However, he claimed he wasn't aware of the other woman he flirted with was married. I told him to check for a wedding ring next time. I questioned him further by asking why he escaped heaven. His response was heartwarming. He thought that by entering the world of the living, he could win money gambling and thus help those in poverty. Unfortunately, his plan backfired as he lost money. He was over his head in debt and made a deal with the loan shark. I told him that the world would eventually work out their problems. Though, in the meantime, he was better off in heaven.

I took a break to eat the meal being served, followed by a nap. When I awoke, the train was still rolling. It was time for Emma to have my full undivided attention. I explained that in order to graduate into heaven, it was mandatory to pass five major classes. The subjects of the study were forgiveness, friendliness, music, giving, and love. I informed Emma that her first course of action would be to check-in at reservations on the first floor. She felt insecure with a lack of self-confidence. I assured her that I would stay by her side every step of the way.

CHAPTER 31

Matthew and I only had a short time to talk on the train. He said it was apparent that I needed to learn my lessons for myself. I had a bit of a stubborn and self-assured character. It was true that I didn't always follow words of advice. Though, I enjoyed my time in heaven and my extra time with Matthew. It was better than being home alone, merely surviving.

Upon the ghost train's arrival at Heaven's Station, thirty ghosts were waiting outside to board. I explained to Emma that the ghosts had most likely failed a class leading to heaven. It was routine protocol for ghosts to reboard the ghost train if they didn't pass a class. They were then assigned someone to help before returning to the station.

I departed from Matthew once again. I was never too good at planning for the long term. However, parting from Matthew was especially more difficult this time. Thus, I began to wonder if I could find a way to be with him every day. *"Maybe I can speak to God about hiring me for a position onboard the ghost train,"* I thought. I decided that after I was done showing Emma the ropes, I would enter heaven and talk to God directly.

Matthew and I embraced as we said our goodbyes. I gave him a kiss and exited the train. Emma followed close behind. She commented that my relationship was like a love story. I told her I was glad she was with me as I could use the moral support. She could see on my face how hard it was to leave Matthew.

"You have a friend in me," said Emma.

"Likewise," I added.

When I opened the main lobby door, and we both entered, the All Saints Band greeted us with rock music. The ambiance was electrifying. All of the ghosts wore formal suits and dresses. There were gourmet snacks and decorations of streamers and balloons. As Emma's friend and mentor, I needed to explain the reason for the celebration.

"It's not always like this here. Usually, the atmosphere is casual and relaxed. Matthew must have notified them I was on my way. You see, my name is featured at the Hall of Fame on the twelfth floor. I helped save the world, so now I am considered a celebrity here," I said.

I then told Emma to follow me to the reservations counter.

"Give them your name," I instructed her.

Emma gave the reservations clerk her name. The clerk took over ten minutes, searching for Emma in the computer system.

"I found it. According to the documents, we have been expecting you since 1898," said the clerk to Emma.
"Yes, she's late in more ways than one," I joked.

Unfortunately, my sense of humor isn't always appreciated. The clerk told me to step back and mind my own business. It was apparent she was unaware of my celebrity status.

The reservations clerk handed Emma a card with directions to her classes. I told Emma that I could answer any questions she had. She was curious about the special guest that was printed at the top of her reservation card.

"Who is the special guest?" Emma asked me.

I simply smiled and gave her a wink. I thought the answer was obvious since Emma saw how I was greeted. I knew it would eventually click, and she'd figure it out.

There was enough time for me to show Emma around the first floor. I led her down a hallway and highlighted the student library and cafe. I was astonished when Emma said that heaven was extraordinary.

"This isn't heaven, Emma. There are no words to describe the unbelievable promised land. You don't actually enter the gates of heaven until you reach the seventh floor. Your classes are on floors 2 - 6. Your first class is Forgiveness Training 101 on Floor 2. Speaking of which, we need to get there now. Your class is about to begin. Don't worry. I'll be with you," I informed her.

As we waited for the elevator, I thought, *"I guess it makes sense that Emma thought we were already in heaven. She had never seen electricity, an elevator, or heard rock music."*

Emma and I hopped on the elevator and rode up to Floor 2. She was soon to meet Mrs. Griver-Wright, her first ghostly teacher. I felt a sense of reward, guiding Emma on her journey towards heaven.

CHAPTER 32

Emma and I made it to Forgiveness Training one minute before the bell rang. Each time the ghosts heard the sound of the bell, they applauded. It was common knowledge that the ringing of a bell meant an angel got its wings. I wasn't going to let them know that it was possible to simply buy wings in heaven. I suppose it all made sense since the cash register bell rang after every purchase.

The classroom was packed, so Emma and I were fortunate to find two available front-row desks. We darted to our seats just in time. Mrs. Griver-Wright began by welcoming me back. She then informed the class that it was an important day and asked the special guest to please stand. It was a pleasure to be honored in this manner.

As I began to stand, the ghosts all turned toward the back of the classroom and applauded. I turned back to look as well. To my amazement, God was there standing up, wearing a suit and tie. Mrs. Griver-Wright introduced Him to the class.

"Class, you have the unique opportunity to meet God ahead of your arrival to heaven. He will be teaching today," she informed the students.

The teacher then addressed God.

"It isn't necessary for you to sit in the back of the classroom. Please come up to the front," said Mrs. Griver-Wright.
"Thank you. I like to sit in the back to keep a watch on everyone," said God as He made his way to the front of the classroom to teach.

God started by saying the celebration was a kind gesture, although the formal attire was unnecessary. He was looking forward to returning to heaven, where He wore comfortable clothes. God then began His lesson.

"Look, class, everyone has their own ideas and beliefs, so I am going to speak in the moral aspects of forgiveness. Disregard religion for a moment. In fact, I realize referring to me as God is distressing to some. Therefore, you can call me "Mr. Jones.""

I raised my hand in an attempt to lighten the subject.

"Does that mean we need to keep up with the Jones?" I joked after being called upon.

"Actually, that's a very good question, Adalyn. The answer is 'Yes.' You should always strive to be your absolute best. I can be viewed as a role model. Try to keep up with me. You will never achieve perfectionism. However, continually striving for improvement will bring rewards."

"Thank you," I said in return.

"On with the lesson. Forgiving others who repent and seek forgiveness brings a sense of peace. I love everyone. It can be hard to forgive and take some time," He said.

I raised my hand again.

"Some sins are horrific. How can we forgive everything?" I asked.

"Referring back to your original question, keep up with The Jones. I have forgiven the worst of sins. If I can do it, so can you. I have created you with the ability to make decisions, so the choice is ultimately yours," He said.

God asked if there were any more questions. No one raised their hand. God went on to give examples of people and situations He forgave. His lesson lasted forty minutes. He had enough time to tell us to take slow, deep breaths in order to relax our bodies and minds. He ended by saying forgiveness blesses the soul.

Mrs. Griver-Wright then handed out tests on the day's lesson. Most of it was multiple choice. However, there was a section to write a short essay. We were to write about someone from our lives who we needed to forgive. I wrote that I needed to forgive myself. I had cut many ties with people for no reason and never again reached out. I then took a slow, deep breath and asked myself for forgiveness.

Both the teacher and God corrected our tests as the students socialized among themselves. Emma and I had a short conversation with the ghostly man sitting next to her. He said that he wasn't certain God was real.

"How do I know that He is really God and that God really exists," the ghostly man asked me.

"He's right here in this classroom so you can see He does exist. Miracles in life happen through Him. You made it from death to Heaven's Station, didn't you? There's more beyond here that there are no words for. Heaven is awesome. If you don't believe it, I suppose you will see for yourself. In the meantime, have faith," I replied.

The tests were finished being graded. The cards handed to each student said either "Pass" or "Fail." God is the best teacher because every student passed. The class then ended, and I was hoping to get the chance to talk to God in the hallway. However, He was busy preparing for the next class. Hence, Emma and I walked to Friendliness Training 101 together.

CHAPTER 33

Emma and I walked into the friendliness classroom with time to spare. As Emma's mentor, I thought my actions would be more educational than my words. Therefore, I displayed a bright smile and greeted the ghostly teacher with a "Hello." Additionally, I courteously waved to the ghostly students. The teacher, Mrs. Kindly, noticed my commendable behavior, although she chose not to shine the spotlight on me.

As the students got situated, God walked into the room. The class applauded as He approached the front to teach. Mrs. Kindly was aware we had already had the pleasure of meeting Him. Therefore, she took a seat and let Him lead the day's lesson.

God began by stating that being friendly is effortless. Nonetheless, He said some make it difficult.

"Not everyone passes this class," He said.

He went on to advise us to make a concerted effort to smile and treat one another with kindness.

"I understand there are times when you feel miserable or angry. However, I want you to learn to set negative emotions aside when you are dealing with someone else. Then during your time alone, embrace those emotions, and work through them. Get support from others when you have difficulty with this. The more ideal scenario is to learn how to be friendly at the same time you are feeling bad. It is possible to experience negative emotions and still show kindness to others," God said.

I felt pride when Emma followed my lead and raised her hand. God asked her to speak.

"Some pick fights whether you're being kind or not. So, if you're fighting with someone, you have to be kind?" asked Emma.
"I do understand that scenario. Those that provoke for no good reason will get their day," He surprisingly said.
"Karma?" asked Emma.
"Therapy," answered God.

He further explained that therapy offices are located on the floors underneath heaven. Some ghosts are required to attend before taking classes. It delays their potential entrance into heaven, although it is well worth the outcome. Everyone who enters the gates of heaven is suited to be an angel and has truly earned the angelic status.

"Not everyone gets alone time to think through their emotions," said one of the ghostly students.
"As I stated, that would be the ideal measure. The bottom line is to always strive to be your best. Take care of yourself physically, mentally, emotionally, and spiritually. Be kind to others. Help those in need," God replied.

God said that the class was delightfully challenging. He was pleased that we engaged in his lessons. Mrs. Kindly then handed out the test. I was stunned to see only one question. I raised my hand to confirm that there wasn't more to the test.

"God and I collaborated ahead of today. We decided to be kind and ask only one question," stated Mrs. Kindly.
"Thank you," I replied.

The question asked to write down the one most important lesson that was taught. I wrote to always strive to be your best. I must have been correct since I passed, as did the entire class.

To my surprise, God approached me after class was done. He wanted to know why I was taking these classes again.

"You passed all five classes before," He said.

It was strange to answer God knowing He already knew the answer. He is the All-Knowing God. Nonetheless, I respectfully answered.

"I am not only mentoring Emma, but I am retaking the classes for extra credit," I said.

"I broke the mold when I made you, Adalyn," God added.

Emma and I said "farewell" to Mrs. Kindly and continued to Music class. I was looking forward to seeing the teacher, Mrs. Harper, once again. She was always my favorite. I was certain Emma would like her as well.

CHAPTER 34

The music class was a blast! Upon our arrival, Emma and I walked into a classroom full of musical instruments. There was a grand piano, a drum set, and small instruments such as a tambourine and maracas. The desks had been removed and replaced with congas and bongos by each chair. There was even a microphone connected to a speaker.

Mrs. Harper wasted no time getting the class started. She instructed the class to bang away on the congas and bongos. We all tried to keep the same beat. One ghostly student led the group by first lightly tapping the conga. The class joined in with light taps that increased to loud banging. My heart rate increased as it required increased strength and endurance over time.

The class took a break from drumming to listen to God. It was shocking to learn that He played the drums in a rock band. I had always assumed He only liked worship music. God stated that he did, indeed, appreciate worship music, although He had a warm preference for rock.

God picked up the drumsticks and took a seat at the drum set. He must have summoned angels from heaven because four angels entered the room. I had seen them in class before. Their names spelled out, "Noel." They were the angels, Nora, Olivia, Elliott, and Leon. It turned out that they were members of God's band. It was obvious they hadn't been notified of the dress code that day. The four angels were wearing jeans and t-shirts and chose not to wear their wings.

Nora took the microphone, and Olivia brought her own bass guitar, and Elliot had his own electric guitar. After Leon sat down at the piano,

God's band began playing. It was thunderous and electrifying. The class joined in playing the congas and bongos. We had a lot of fun.

I raised my hand after the music stopped. God motioned me to speak.

"What's the name of your band?" I asked.
"Mr. Jones and the Noels," replied God.
"All of your music sounds like number one hits," I added.
"Thank you, Adalyn. We're so loud in heaven that the sounds from our band create thunder and lightning. Don't believe that myth that I'm up in heaven bowling. In fact, it's not a sport I am particularly fond of. There is a striking story behind my dislike of bowling, but I'll spare telling you. I'm afraid you would all split from class." God wittingly said.

It was a refreshing privilege to incur a glimpse of God's humorous side. Mrs. Harper handed out the tests. There were three questions and room to write whatever we desired. The questions were:

- Did you have fun in music class today?
- Are you always trying your best?
- Did you learn anything in music class today?

I answered the questions and wrote that the band was awesome. I had momentarily forgotten I was there as a mentor. While the tests were being graded, I asked Emma if she had any questions for me. She replied that she only had a comment. Emma thanked me for pulling her out of her dark world and bringing her to Heaven's Station. She said she couldn't wait to enter heaven and listen to more of God's band. I believed that Emma had caught rock fever.

Our test scores were handed out. Once again, the entire class passed. It was time to head to Giving Training 101, taught by Professor Wright. Emma and I exited the music room and walked to the elevator. The ghosts and I waited in anticipation of the following class.

CHAPTER 35

Professor Wright, the giving teacher, was married to Mrs. Griver-Wright. They met each other at the school leading to heaven. They were ghosts that never entered the gate of heaven themselves. Professor Wright and Mrs. Griver-Wright had foregone the experience in order to teach. It was an unselfish sacrifice that all of the teachers made. Their time spent teaching was a lesson in giving within itself.

God entered the room, and the class applauded. He stood up front as Professor Wright took a seat. God began His lesson by listing examples of giving. There were ten items referred to as the "5 Me's" as follows:

- Money
- Ear-to-ear smiles

- Material items
- Endless inspiration and hope

- Meals
- Eternal friendship

- Much time
- Ernest advice

- Many blessings
- Enjoyment and laughter

God then taught that giving is self-rewarding. It brings a sense of pride and peace within oneself to give to someone else. A ghostly student raised his hand. God addressed him to speak.

"Mr. Jones, Sir, what if someone takes more than they deserve?" asked the student.

"You have faith in the outcome," God responded.

"What if I'm robbed of everything I own?" the student went on to ask.

"Being robbed and giving are two different topics. This class does like to challenge me with questions. Pray for those who steal from you and give to those who deserve your generosity," said God.

"Thank you," said the student.

"Remember, those are ten examples. There are thousands of ways to give," God added.

He went on to teach us that we should always acknowledge those who give to us. We learned to be grateful and count our blessings every day. Professor Wright handed out the tests. One of the questions asked us to state one thing we had given. I wrote, "my heart."

Everyone in the class received a passing grade. Our next class was Love Training 101. Emma and I headed to the elevator.

CHAPTER 36

Love was my favorite subject. I had failed the class the first time. Thus I was sent back down to ride the ghost train. I was to help someone, which, as I said before, was routine protocol. I believe the person I was to help was myself. Afterwards, I repeated the class of love with a passing grade. I was to graduate into heaven. Instead, I chose to ride the ghost train in search of my home.

It was surprising that there wasn't a teacher for Love Training besides God. Mr. Robinson, my former teacher, had retired. I asked a few of the ghosts for information on the whereabouts of the teacher. They said the rumor was that no one wanted the job. I had previously taught the class as a temporary replacement. I had assumed a new teacher had been hired.

God began His lesson by teaching that the heart has no choice who it loves. He understood how much heartache there was in the world. Still, He emphasized the beauty of love. He went on to discuss the richest treasure being the gift of love.

"Heartache is a beautiful thing. It shows the depth of your ability to give love. I notice all heartbreaks and suffering. It is important to pray," said God.

The ghosts in class appeared somber. They all looked heartbroken, including Emma. I believed I was the only one who was happily in love. No one even challenged God with questions.

The tests were readily handed out. I was shocked when the results were handed back. Everyone in the class received a passing grade, with the exception of Emma. I had thought that my love for Matthew was leading by example. I was puzzled as to the reason for Emma's failing grade. Nevertheless, she was required to board the ghost train and help someone.

When class ended, I had a chance to talk directly to God.

"Hello, Mr. Jones," I said, addressing The Almighty God.
"Adalyn, it's been a pleasure having you in classes today," He said.
"Thank you. It has been an honor having you as a teacher as well. I am curious about a couple of things," I said.
"You know you can always ask me anything. What's on your mind," He asked.
"Who has been teaching this class since Mr. Robinson left?" I asked.
"It's heartening that you are concerned enough to ask. The other teachers have been taking turns filling in temporarily. I'm certain the position will be filled soon," He said.
"I would apply for the position, but I have something else in mind. In fact, I was hoping to have an opportunity to ask you directly," I said.
"Go ahead. Ask away," God said.
"Is it possible for me to work on the ghost train? I realize there isn't a current opening, though. Couldn't you create a new position? I miss Matthew so much. I need to be with him every day. Maybe I could be the train's janitor," I said.

My janitor's suggestion gave God a chuckle. He stated that He had bigger plans for me. Although, He didn't elaborate. He assured me I would find my life's path. I was hoping to gain more insight, but He simply told me to keep the faith. I could see He wasn't going to give me any more information, so I moved the focus off of myself.

"How is the situation in heaven with the workers' strike?" I asked.
"It was a bit chaotic when I returned from vacation. I got everything under control immediately. Stella is up there filling in for me again, but this time only for a day. You do understand that no matter where I

am located, I am always with you, right? I never truly go on vacation," God said.

"Yes, I understand," I replied.

God and I bid each other farewell. I didn't get the vibe that God was going to create a job for me on board the ghost train. I had renewed faith that my life would turn out fine in spite of letting Emma down. I felt as though I had failed as a mentor. Although, I was not about to give up on her. I told Emma that I was a loyal friend and would remain by her side. Both of us headed to the elevator. As the ghosts waited for the elevator to go up, I pressed the "down" button. Emma and I were headed back to the ghost train.

CHAPTER 37

Emma's failure was bittersweet. She was not able to enter the gates of heaven. Whereas I would have another opportunity to re-engage with Matthew.

Emma's ticket was waiting for her at the ticket counter of Heaven's Station. However, there was no ticket for me. Nevertheless, Matthew permitted me on board the train. He was elated to see me once again. Once the ghostly passengers and I got situated in our seats, the train began rolling. Matthew then made his way down the aisle to talk.

"I see you've come to your senses," he said to me.

"I'm not sure I know what you're referring to," I said with curiosity.

"You're going home. I'm happy you listened, and you're leaving heaven to live life," Matthew said.

I was surprised that Matthew thought I was going home. I thought he would have the desire to spend as much time with me as possible. I had to let him know the truth.

"Um, Matthew, I hate to break it to you, but I'm not headed home. Emma failed a class, so I'm acting as her mentor as she helps someone," I informed him.

"I see. I wish you and Emma the best with that. Speaking of which, I am about to announce instructions to all ghosts on board about the televisions," said Matthew.

On the back of each seat was a television. It was to only be used to find out who you were to help. Matthew walked back to the front to speak to everyone. He told the ghosts to put their headphones on and turn on their televisions. I watched as Emma turned her t.v. on. However, she had technical difficulties. There was only static on the screen. I asked Emma to allow me to use her headphones so that I could correct the situation. I then pressed the button for technical support.

"May I help you?" said a voice from technical support.
"Yes. We're having some technical difficulties with the television on board the ghost train. It is only displaying static with white noise," I said.
"Give me a moment to work on it, ma'am," said the voice.

Emma and I waited for five minutes. The voice returned, saying that there was nothing that could be done. I thought that my celebrity status would help.

"Do you know who I am?" I asked the technician.
"No. Should I?" said the technician.
"Adalyn. I am featured in the Hall of Fame for saving the world," I said with enormous pride.
"I'm sorry, ma'am. There is nothing that can be done," the technician repeated.

I had only one other course of action.

"I'll be sure to talk to my good friend, Lenny Deter, about this," I said.
"Oh, Mr. Deter? Give me a minute. I think I can fix the problem," said the technician.

Just like magic, the technical problem was resolved. I had never known anyone important that I could use name dropping with before. It felt powerful. I handed the headphones back to Emma so she could find out who she was to help. I glanced at her screen to view information about the person. It read:

- Name: River Wilson
- Age: 26
- Location: Flower City, New York
- Problem: Depressed and Heartbroken

I couldn't believe my eyes. River was the daughter of an old friend of mine, Sabrina Wilson. I severed ties with Sabrina years prior for no reason. In fact, I had dissed all of my friends over the years. I hadn't seen River since she was a baby.

"Thank you for getting the technical issue fixed," said Emma.
"You're welcome," I politely replied.
"I'm supposed to help River Wilson, someone I don't know," said Emma.
"We can do the job together!" I exclaimed.
"How am I supposed to help someone who is depressed and heartbroken when I can't even pass Love Training 101?" asked Emma.
"I was the first ever to fail the class. You must be the second. Looks like we're a pair. God has us on this mission for a purpose Emma. He has a reason for everything. Maybe I'm your mentor because I overcame my broken heart. Was your heart broken, Emma?" I asked.
"Not in the slightest. I never formed any lasting relationships. I didn't have a broken heart. I broke others' hearts," Emma replied.
"I see. You left people before they could leave you. I did the same thing. Maybe God's plan is for you to see River Wilson with a broken heart for a reason," I said.

The train came to a halt. It was time for Emma and me to exit the train and help heal a broken heart.

CHAPTER 38

Emma and I left the Ghost Train Station and crossed Gray Street. We walked until we reached the Flower City Express. Matthew had handed me money before we parted, so I was able to purchase a ticket to ride into Flower City.

Emma and I sat down next to each other on the crowded train. It was only a short ride into Flower City, yet quite a bit was said. I wasn't expecting Emma to delve into my life as she did. I had hoped that no one would think I was talking to myself, being that Emma could not be seen.

"So, who broke your heart?" asked Emma.
"No one broke my heart," I replied.
"Umm, but you said your broken heart had healed earlier. Who broke it, Adalyn?" Emma asked once more.

I paused for a brief moment. I wasn't sure how to respond. Suddenly out of the blue, Lenny appeared.

"Go ahead, Angel. Tell her," said Lenny.

I was shocked to see Lenny. God had sent him back to heaven the last I knew. I felt as though Lenny and Emma were ganging up on me. Besides, how would Lenny know who broke my heart? It appeared that he already knew the answer. I looked straight into Lenny's eyes and then turned to Emma to speak. I really was not prepared to respond.

"Just someone from my past. It's not important. We all get a broken heart at least once. It's part of life. That is why we need to help River Wilson. She is suffering from pain. It is our mission to save her from her heartache. We need to ...," I said before being interrupted.

"There's the Adalyn, or should I say Angel that I know —always rambling on when she's nervous," said Lenny.

"Lenny, how did you even get here? I mean, why? God sent you back to heaven," I said.

"Angel, if there are any lessons to be learned thus far, it is that best friends have each other's backs. I am not going to let you hide your pain and suffering forever. It is true —you're both on a mission to help River pull out of her depression. But Angel, maybe it's time for you to save you," said Lenny.

Lenny knew me better than I realized. I was suffering deep inside. It was true that I had reunited with Matthew, the love of my life. Yet, I had never really healed my own broken heart. And that was something I was able to hide from the entire world with the exception of one angel —Leonard Calvin Deter, my best friend, Lenny.

Before anything more could be said, the Flower City Express had arrived in Flower City. Emma and I were off to help River Wilson with her broken heart. Lenny tagged along.

Since I was alive, I was obviously visible to other people. As well, Lenny being an angel, was also visible. However, the ghost, Emma, could not be seen by others. I was never quite sure why I had the ability to see ghosts. *I wondered to myself if there was a way to make it so that people could see Emma. It was an important part of the plan to help River.*

"Lenny, you know everything. How do we change Emma's appearance from a ghost to a living human being? Isn't there something you can do?" I asked.

"First of all, for what reason?" asked Lenny.

"Well, I have somewhat of a plan to help River, but Emma has to be involved and not an invisible bystander," I informed him.

Without warning, Maurice appeared.

"Club 777 V.I.P. member at your service," said Maurice as he handed me his business card.

"Maurice! What are you doing here?" I said with excitement.

"You need help. I am your guardian angel. It is as simple as that. Now let me see if I have this straight. You need Emma, the ghost, to appear as though a living human being in order to help a living human being. Correct?" said Maurice.

"That is absolutely right. How did you know, and how are you going to be able to help?" I asked.

"Your first question doesn't really need answering. I am your guardian angel. How can I help, you ask? Check out my business card.

Maurice's business card read: "Club 777. Where Magic Begins and Ends. Maurice W. Winters. V.I.P. Member."

"I'm a magician as well," said Maurice.

"What?!" I exclaimed.

"Hocus pocus, alakazam, make Emma look alive," he said as he waved a magic wand.

Suddenly, Emma turned from looking like a white ghost with white hair to appearing just as I did —a living human being.

"So, people will be able to see her now?" I asked Maurice.

"Yes, ma'am. Everyone and anyone. Anything else you need while I'm here?" he asked me.

"Yes. An answer to my question. How much time do you spend at Club 777? I mean, you're supposed to be protecting me at all times," I said with concern.

"Adalyn, what have I told you time after time? I am with you always in spirit," said Maurice.

"I know. But you seem to do better when you're not distracted with other things," I said.

"Are you complaining about my services?" he asked.

"Oh, no, not at all. I apologize if I made it appear so. I am ever grateful to you and thank you for helping me out this time," I said in a hurry.

I began to feel a bit of shame for what I said. Maurice had come through for me more than once. It wasn't his fault he had a gambling addiction. I then told myself to begin appreciating more instead of pointing out flaws. It was a lesson to myself.

Maurice was in a rush to return to heaven. He said there was a dance at the club that night and that he had asked a special lady friend to go along with him. I wished him a good night, and he disappeared. Lenny, Emma, and I were ready to help change the fate of one person in need—River Wilson.

CHAPTER 39

The three of us, Emma, Lenny, and I, traveled to the home of River Wilson. She lived with her mother, my old friend, Sabrina Wilson. I was hesitant to ring the doorbell and be confronted with River's mother. I guess I stood in thought too long because Lenny took over and knocked on the door. Sure enough, Sabrina opened the door with a look of wonderment.

"Can I help you?" asked Sabrina.

I knew I had to say something. It was obvious she didn't recognize me. She must have been confused as to why three people were at her door, and none of us were saying anything. And, if we had said we were there to help her daughter, River, I think she would have slammed the door in our faces.

"Sabrina, it's me, Adalyn. Your old friend from work at Powers Corporation," I informed her.

"Oh my gosh! Adalyn. I didn't recognize you. I guess we all age," she responded.

Sabrina wasn't helping my ego. I thought I looked young for my age. Everyone told me that. However it had been many years since we had seen one another. I suppose I did look different than my working years. As a matter of fact, I was about thirty years old when I severed ties with Sabrina. However, that was beside the point. I had to come up with a reason why the three of us were standing outside her door. And I had to come up with the reason fast.

"Sabrina, let me introduce you to my friends, Emma and Lenny," I first said.

"It's a pleasure to meet you both," Sabrina said politely.

"As well, the pleasure is ours," Lenny replied.

"What brings you here, Adalyn? Come inside for a while," said Sabrina.

The three of us stepped inside Sabrina's house. It was immaculate. Sabrina led us to the living room, where we all took a seat. She then addressed me once again.

"Is there anything I can do for you?" asked Sabrina.

"Oh, well, umm, I'm having a party. I thought I would get old friends together. You know, people we haven't seen in ages," I reluctantly said.

"What a wonderful idea," she responded.

Just then, a young girl in her twenties walked by the living room. She was wearing sweatpants and a sweatshirt, her hair was in tatters, and she appeared to be depressed. I had assumed she was River. Just then, Sabrina raised her voice an octave and addressed the young woman.

"River, please come in here. I have someone here that I want you to meet," said Sabrina to her daughter.

I wasn't sure how this was all going to play out. After all, Emma, Lenny, and I were on a mission to help River. We were only just being introduced to her. To my surprise, Emma knew just what to say.

"It's nice to meet you, River. You have a unique name. I'll bet it matches your heart," said Emma.

"Thank you," replied River with a look of discomfort, not knowing any of us.

"Your mother and Adalyn are old friends. Adalyn is a good friend of mine. She's here to get reacquainted and invite your mother to a get-together. She's having a party. You're invited too, River," Emma said.

"Oh, that's nice. I'm not really up to going to a party, though. But thank you anyway," replied River.

"I understand. I'm not up to parties myself either right now. I'm trying to get over the loss of my boyfriend," said Emma.

"Oh, I'm sorry for your loss. Did he pass away recently?" asked River.

"River, that's really not our business," Sabrina interrupted.

"Oh, it's fine, Sabrina. She didn't say anything wrong. My boyfriend isn't dead. He left me for another woman. He shattered my heart into pieces," Emma said.

I was a bit confused. Emma had said that she was the one who broke hearts and that she had never had her heart broken. I made a mental note to myself to question her about this for clarification later. In the meantime, I could see that Emma and River had made a real connection. Our lack of having an exact plan seemed to be working.

"I know how that feels —having your heart shattered into pieces," said River, opening up to us.

"Would you mind if I went into the other room to have a small chat with your daughter? It seems we have something in common and, if she feels as bad as I do, I may be able to help," said Emma as she addressed Sabrina.

"Oh, yes, good. Go ahead. It will give me time to catch up with Adalyn," said Sabrina. She then whispered to Emma so that River would not hear and said, "And maybe you can get her out of her moodiness too."

Lenny and I chatted with Sabrina while Emma was consoling River in another room. After an hour, Emma and River returned to the living room. Sabrina addressed her daughter.

"Are you okay? You look as though you have been crying," she said to River.

"I've been healing. Emma really helped me. We cried and laughed together. I think maybe I will go to Adalyn's party," said River to her mother with a smile.

It was time to leave. Sabrina thanked me for coming over and said that she hadn't seen her daughter smile in months. She couldn't stop thanking Emma. As Lenny, Emma, and I were walking out the door, Sabrina had a question for me.

"When and where is the party?" she asked.

Once again, I had to do some quick thinking.

"It will be at my house sometime around Christmas. I'll let you know," I again said with reluctance.
"Here's my phone number. Don't become a stranger this time," said Sabrina to me.
"Oh, I won't. I'll be sure to call," I said as the three of us left.

Lenny, Emma, and I headed back to the ghost train. We first rode the Flower City Express to the outskirts of the city, exited the train, and crossed Gray Street to board the ghost train. I had a question for both Lenny and Emma. I was going to address the two of them on the train.

CHAPTER 40

Matthew allowed me to board the ghost train, once again, without a ticket. It was so good to see him. He was busy as the train was crowded more than usual. Nevertheless, he took the time to give me a big welcoming hug. I then took a seat next to Emma with Lenny across the aisle from us. It was time to ask my questions.

"Okay, I have a question for both of you —first, the easy one. Lenny, I know you said you have my back, and you couldn't stand to be in heaven as you watched me suffer heartache. My question is, how did you get past God? He had told you to return to heaven," I said with curiosity.

"God could see it in my eyes. I approached Him directly. I said, 'I need to help my best friend, Adalyn. She is in deep pain.' He knew. Without hesitation, He told me to go do what I needed to do," said Lenny.

"You addressed me as Adalyn? But you call me Angel," I said.

"I'm sorry, Angel. I was afraid that if I used the name Angel, God wouldn't know who I was talking about. He knows a lot of angels," Lenny said in an attempt to be humorous.

"I see. Very funny. Okay. Now your turn Emma," I said as I turned towards her.

"Oh, no. What's this about?" asked Emma.

"First, you say you've never had a broken heart. Then you go and tell River that your heart was shattered into pieces. I'm confused. Which is it, Emma?" I asked with demand a for an answer.

"Adalyn, I made up the story. No man ever broke my heart. Maybe if I had lived longer, someone would have had the chance. But it never happened. I told River a story that she could relate to in order to help pull her out of her misery. I believe I succeeded," Emma proudly said.

"I believe, indeed, you did," I replied.

My questions had both been answered as the train rolled along. Matthew then approached me. Again, he wanted to know why I did not stay in Flower City. I guess he wanted me to go back to the home we shared and live a lonely miserable life. My intentions were to return to heaven with the hopes that I could spend time with Matthew. Even though he had a job as the ghost train conductor, he did have time off.

"Emma and I finished our mission. I got her to the location of the person she was to help, and Emma did just that. I'm on my way back to heaven to inform God that our mission is complete. Emma can now retake the classes and graduate into heaven," I said to Matthew.

"Can't Emma tell God herself?" Matthew asked.

Reluctant to say, Matthew was getting a bit on my nerves. He wasn't at peace with the notion of my perusing heaven. I was not 'living life' as he would say. Nevertheless, I ignored his desires and continued with determination to act as Emma's mentor. After all, I would not only be helping Emma. It was my avenue to get back into heaven.

CHAPTER 41

First, Matthew was beginning to annoy me, and then Emma as well. As I explained to her that I would be at her side when she returned to classes, Emma iterated a lack of need for me. She emphasized that she understood the procedures by that point and that she did not need a mentor. *What would I do? I thought to myself. I needed an excuse to get back into heaven. I would just have to find another way or lie to Emma. I could tell her that God insisted I continue to act as her mentor. Lenny could help me decide.*

"What would Lenny do in this situation?" I asked him.

"You don't want to know what Lenny would do. You need to ask yourself, 'What would Adalyn do?'" said Lenny.

"Oh yeah. I know what you would do. You would simply break into heaven. So, I guess the answer is I should lie to Emma," I said.

"Okay. I see that you actually do need my help. Lying isn't exactly the best way to get yourself into heaven, Angel. Most people try to not lie in order to get there," Lenny said with a chuckle.

"I'm glad you see the humor in all of this," I sarcastically said.

"There's no need to get emotional. I'll take care of things," said Lenny.

By this time, Emma, Lenny, and I had entered the lobby of Heaven's Station. I had parted from Matthew with a hug and kiss; although, my emotions were numb. I didn't have the exciting feeling of being close to him. I thought it was strange, but I disregarded it from my mind. I was tired from all of the traveling, so I took a seat in the lobby. Lenny then tugged on Emma's arm to draw her away from the reservations desk. The two of them chatted with one another as I sat staring in a daze with exhaustion.

"It's all set," Lenny said as he approached me.

"What happened? What did you say to Emma?" I asked.

"I used my magical charm. You'll continue to mentor her," Lenny said with a wink.

"Maybe I shouldn't ask this, but what exactly was said?" I again asked.

"I played on her sympathies and told Emma that you needed her more than she needed you," said Lenny.

It was all set, as Lenny had said. He had even talked with the reservations clerk to inform her that I was a V.I.P. and had all rights to enter the classrooms. Lenny, Emma, and I headed to the elevator to ride to the second floor. Emma had misunderstood one important procedure. She thought that since she only failed Love Training 101, she would only need to repeat that class. Lenny and I both informed her that it was mandatory for her to repeat all of the classes.

"It isn't easy to get into heaven, is it?" Emma said.

"No one said it was easy; however, it is worth every bit of effort put forth. You will never look back in anger, bitterness, or regret," Lenny informed her.

I sat by Emma's side in each classroom as her mentor, and Lenny stood by as my friend. It was no surprise that Emma again passed the classes in forgiveness, friendliness, music, and giving. It was a surprise, however, that no one questioned Emma as to her new appearance as a living human being. The first time she took classes, she was a white ghost with white hair. Yet, as I said, neither Emma's ghostly teachers nor ghostly classmates made a comment.

Emma's pass or fail grade in the final class, Love Training, would determine our next course of action. She passed Love Training with flying colors. Lenny, Emma, and I made some dance moves outside the classroom afterward. We were ready to celebrate and enter heaven.

CHAPTER 42

Since graduations into heaven occurred on Saturdays and it was Friday afternoon, Lenny, Emma, and I had time to spare. We were each assigned a bed and a desk on the basement level to use at our convenience. Lenny naturally had a different plan. He wanted to return to Flower City for the night to "paint the town," as he said. Emma asked what color we were going to paint it. Lenny and I both laughed. Due to being from an earlier century, she had never heard the term.

I didn't think Lenny's plan was a particularly good idea. After all, in the whole scheme of things, we really didn't have that much time on our hands. We would have to board the ghost train and travel to the Ghost Train Station across the street from the Flower City Express Station. From there, we would hop on the Flower City Express to where we would enter the city of the living. According to Lenny's plan, our next course of action would be to find a dance hall or bar with music. At that point, we would "paint the town" and then have to return to Heaven's Station. I wondered when I would get some sleep.

"Come on, Angel. It'll be fun. We'll dance, we'll sing, we'll laugh the night away," insisted Lenny as he tried convincing me to go on his venture.

I thought about his so-called brilliant idea for several minutes. *"It would give me a chance to see Matthew on the train again. Maybe I could even get some sleep during the ride," I said to myself.*

"Okay, Lenny. You're getting your way. Emma, are you in agreement with this?" I asked.

"It will be thrilling. People will see that I don't look like a ghost, and it will be as though I am alive again!" she replied.

The three of us hopped on the ghost train on our way to Flower City. Matthew gave me a loving, welcoming hug after boarding the train. It was strange that I still felt numb inside. Though, once again, I disregarded it and went on to explain to Matthew our reason for returning to the train. I assured him that I would be returning home after Emma's graduation ceremony.

I was able to catch up on my sleep on board the train. When our traveling was done, Lenny, Emma, and I ended up at a restaurant with a live band playing. Just ahead of finding the restaurant, we stopped to buy Emma's clothes to fit the era. She looked like a beauty queen. I had to stop myself from being jealous.

"You're just as beautiful," said Lenny.
"Thank you," I replied.

I hadn't said a word to Lenny about what I was thinking. Yet, somehow, he knew. I guess best friends have that ability at times.

In front of the band at the restaurant was a dance floor. Lenny asked me for a dance, and I had the time of my life. We danced to song after song. Emma decided to sit and watch for a while since she had no clue of how dancing was done in the twenty-first century.

Suddenly, Lenny stopped dancing and walked away. I immediately followed behind. He was checking up on Emma because she was talking to a stranger. Lenny turned to me and said that the man had been talking with her during the past five songs. Lenny broke into their conversation.

"Hello, I'm Lenny. And who do I have the pleasure of meeting?" Lenny said to the man.
"This is my new friend, Alex," said Emma.
"Nice to meet you, Lenny," Alex said as the two bumped elbows.

"And this is Adalyn, my dear friend," Emma said to Alex.
Emma then whispered into my ear, "I'm in love."

I pulled Emma aside and explained that she couldn't be in love that fast. *Maybe it was just a figure of speech,* I then thought. Next, Lenny informed Emma that it was time to leave. I don't think he was too happy about Emma's new friend.

"I'll be right there," Emma said as she walked through the crowded room.

We had no idea where she was headed. The problem was that she never returned. Lenny and I waited fifteen minutes, and Alex eventually walked away too. I was beginning to get worried. Lenny kept cool, calm, and collected even though I knew he was panicked.

Lenny and I searched throughout the crowded restaurant, yet there was no sign of Emma. We finally went outside and found her a few blocks down. We weren't sure if we should yell at her or give her a hug. I chose to give her a hug. Lenny chose to give her a lecture.

"You can't just run off like that without us. We're not even supposed to be here. Do you know how much trouble we could have been in if we hadn't found you?" said Lenny to Emma.

"I want to stay here. I know I could be happy here. I met the man of my dreams," Emma explained.

"You can't stay here," Lenny said.

Just then, a wise guy walked by and said, "Hey fella, hey lady, who are you talking to? A ghost?"

At first, I wondered how he knew that Emma was a ghost. Lenny and I then realized that Emma had suddenly returned to her white-ghostly self. It was apparent that no one but us could see her. Maurice's magic had worn off. Emma had a look of sadness all over her face.

"There's nothing to be sad about. Just wait until you get to heaven. You will never be sad again," I said to console her.

"Speaking of which, we need to get back for Emma's graduation," said Lenny.

Thunder and rain began during our trip back to Heaven's Station. Lenny and I knew that meant that God's band, Mr. Jones and the Noel's, were up in heaven performing. Emma still appeared to be sad, but happiness was well on its way.

CHAPTER 43

Lenny, Emma, and I arrived at Heaven's Station just in time for the graduation ceremony. We rode the elevator to Floor 7. When the doors to the elevator opened, I was staring at the gates of heaven. They were wide open to allow the graduates inside. As the three of us approached, an angel woman asked us for our tickets. I hadn't thought about needing one. Neither did Lenny. However, Emma had her ticket and handed it to the angel.

"Hi, Lenny," the angel flirtatiously said.

Lenny apparently knew the angel woman. She allowed Lenny into the ceremony without a ticket. Another angel then handed Emma and Lenny a brochure about heaven and the day's event. They both looked back at me as I stood by the gate, shrugging my shoulders and motioning, "What do I do?"

"It's okay. She's an angel —a well-known angel. Adalyn is featured on Floor 12 in the Hall of Fame," Lenny said to the angel in an attempt to get me through the gates. Although, I think the angel was jealous, thinking that I might be Lenny's love interest. The angel refused to allow me inside. Suddenly, God approached.

"Hello, Adalyn, hello, Lenny. Welcome to heaven, Emma," God said to us.

He went on to ask the angel, "Is there some sort of conflict here?"

The angel replied, "Yes, this woman, Adalyn, I guess her name is, does not have a ticket."

"As you may recall, I am Emma's mentor. I was at her side throughout her classes. It would bring me much joy to watch her graduate," I said to God.

"Yes, of course," said God as he handed me an 'All-Day Pass' into heaven.

"Why, thank you, God. You are so kind," I spoke.

"You're welcome, Adalyn. It's nice to see you again. And you too, Lenny. Now, if you will, please excuse me. I have other students to welcome. Enjoy the ceremony," said God.

The three of us simultaneously said, "Thank you, God."

I handed the angel my 'All-Day Pass,' and she let me through with a bit of a sneering look on her face. I disregarded it and walked toward the event. Emma parted ways with Lenny and me. She was to sit among the other students during the ceremony. Lenny and I found chairs for the guests. As we waited for the event to begin, The Noels played some instrumental songs. Lenny then surprised me.

"Are you going to tell me?" Lenny asked.

"Tell you what? What are you referring to?" I asked.

"Who broke your heart? Who are you really in love with?" he points blankly asked.

Lenny saw right through me. No one had ever known me that well. *How would I answer his questions, I thought to myself. Those questions hit the core of my insides. The answers were deeply embedded with no intent to surface.*

"I'm waiting. I can wait all day," he looked at me with his arms folded, his eyebrows raised, and a look of patience waiting for my response. I paused for a moment, sadly bowed my head, and spoke.

"His name was Ricky," I said with a sorrowful voice.

The Masters of Ceremony began to speak into the microphone. He welcomed everyone as the event began, which saved me from having to say anything more. As all of the students walked on stage one by one, God handed them their diplomas and a wings certificate. The certificate was to be used to purchase free wings on the mall floor.

I was unprepared for what happened next. Emma chose to go her separate way after the ceremony. She did not even attend the concert afterward. Emma claimed that she was in a hurry to visit her family. She said she hadn't seen them in over a hundred years. In that instance, she wasn't being sarcastic. Emma no longer needed me. She was off to get the wings to fly on her own. I supposed that was the entire purpose of my mentoring. It was time to let go.

CHAPTER 44

I thought the subject of Ricky had been put to rest. However, I was mistaken. While Lenny and I were the last to leave the graduation ceremony on Floor 7, he nudged me.

"Is Ricky alive or dead?" Lenny bluntly asked with no couth.

I paused for a moment. I was taken back by the spot-on question. I gathered my emotions to respond.

"I have no idea. I haven't seen him in years. He could be dead or alive for all I know," I said with a sigh of relief that I was opening up a buried memory.
"Come with me. I have work to do," Lenny instructed me.
"Where are we going," I asked.
"My old stomping grounds. The technology floor. We need to know Ricky's status—whether he is dead or alive," said Lenny.
"You're breaking into the system again?" I asked.
"Only one more time," he replied.

Lenny and I rode the elevator to Floor 27. He gave me no chance to even speak my mind. Knowing if Ricky was dead or alive made no difference to my life. He hadn't been a part of it for twenty years. I did always wonder how he was doing in life. The thought did cross my mind that he could have passed away. I used to think of him on a daily basis. I got over that. It was then about every week of my life. Ricky's memory would not fade, no matter how much I tried.

As soon as the elevator doors opened onto the technology floor, Lenny was greeted with the utmost respect.

"Hello, Mr. Deter," said an angel woman.
"Good afternoon," Lenny replied.
"How do you do, Mr. Deter," said another angel.
"Good day," Lenny spoke.

Lenny led me to a computer and pulled up a chair for me. He sat down to type. After several minutes, he said he got it.

"You got what?" I asked.
"The password. I'm figuring it out. God changed it," he replied.
"I see. It's beyond me what you're doing," I said.
"So far, I have F-A-T-H-E-R_K-N," said Lenny.
"Father knows best," I said, figuring out God's password.
"That's exactly it, Angel. That works!" Lenny said with excitement.

Lenny continued to type. He was interrupted several times by angels wanting technical help. Lenny was a gentleman and responded politely that he was working on an urgent matter. He told the angels that he would be back to check on things. He was smart not to say exactly when, though.

Lenny entered the information about Ricky and determined that he must still be alive. He was nowhere to be found in the computer system. I let out a sigh of relief. I don't know why it mattered to me, but it was good to know that Ricky was among the living.

"You really loved him, didn't you, Angel?" asked Lenny.

He hit my inner core again with his question. I decided to answer honestly. After all, Lenny was my best friend ever.

"I loved him like no other. Could we put the matter to rest now?" I asked.
"Only if that is your desire," Lenny replied.

"Yes, it is," I said

We both then decided to get a bite to eat. We took the elevator to Floor 24 and, once again, ate at Giovanni's restaurant. The food was delicious. It was as though I hadn't eaten in decades. As we sat eating across from one another, we discussed our next venture. I iterated that I needed to leave heaven as I only had a one-day pass. Lenny had other ideas.

CHAPTER 45

Lenny grabbed my hand and led me back to the elevator. I reminded him a second time that I only had a one-day pass into heaven. However it was as though I was talking to a brick wall. Lenny was not listening to me. If he was, he was ignoring my words.

I decided not to ask where he was taking me. He had never led me astray before. He bent the rules a bit in the past, but it all led to where I was that day —in heaven, where Matthew spent time. After all, Matthew was the entire purpose of my stay in heaven.

"Or are you just comfortable being in heaven?" Lenny asked.
"Lenny! Can you read my thoughts?" I said with my eyes wide open.
"No, Angel. I can't read your thoughts. But your feelings are written all over your face. It's time to enter Floor 82, the Dress-up Studios. We're going to celebrate the autumn season by attending a costume party," he said as we stepped from the elevator onto Floor 82.

There were costumes galore everywhere I looked. It was as though I entered a world of fantasy. I hadn't even realized it was autumn.

"You can be anything you want to be, Angel. What have you always wanted to be?" Lenny asked.
"That's easy. I wish I was as beautiful as a model," I replied.
"You already are," Lenny was adamant in saying.
"I already know I won't win by disagreeing with you. It would be a waste of time. Thank you, Lenny. How about if I dress up as an even more beautiful model?" I said with a smile.

"Wish granted. Let's look at some of the costumes," he said with excitement.

Just then, a lady angel approached, asking if we needed help. She worked at the Dress-up Studios as a consultant. I spent more than an hour with her as I tried on several different styles of dresses and accessories. Lenny sat outside the dressing rooms and commented on each one. His eyes popped wide open with the last dress I tried on. It was a long, red tight-fitting gown that sparkled. Lenny was nearly speechless.

"Absolutely stunning!" he said.
"Why? Thank you," I replied as I turned around in a circle, peering into the mirror.
"We'll take it," Lenny said to the consultant.
"And who are you going to the party as?" asked the consultant.
"Her biggest fan," Lenny replied with a look of sincerity.

The dress-up consultant convinced Lenny that he should at least wear a suit and tie. She found the perfect attire for him on her first try. It was a dark gray suit with a red tie that matched my dress. She even found a top-hat that went well with the suit.

"Are you planning to go to the salon after this?" the consultant asked me.

I hadn't thought about that, but it was a good idea. Lenny and I traveled to Floor 454. I had my hair and makeup done at the salon while Lenny was at the barbershop. An hour later, we were both ready for the party.

CHAPTER 46

On our ride down the elevator to Floor 21, Lenny and I ran into none other than Matthew. He smiled the moment he saw me, gave me a hug and kiss, and asked me where I was going. I didn't know how to answer him since I wasn't even supposed to be going anywhere other than the graduation ceremony. Lenny stepped in and saved the day.

"We're celebrating after attending graduation," he said to Matthew.

"I see. I'd love to join you two, but I'm on my way to speak to God about emergency repair work needed on the ghost train. Enjoy the celebration," Matthew said as he stayed on the elevator to ride to a different floor.

I was a bit saddened. Matthew had not made even one comment about my appearance. I mentioned it to Lenny. His response was that Matthew was married to his job. Lenny again told me I was beautiful and that Matthew was just preoccupied.

The elevator reached Floor 21. When the doors opened, Lenny and I walked out into the autumn scenery. The trees were colorful and majestic. I began to wonder where we were exactly headed wearing costumes.

"There aresome houses just down there," Lenny said as he pointed to a close-by neighborhood made up of what appeared to be mansions, not houses.

"Do you know anyone who lives there?" I asked.

"Of course. My good friend Zander and his wife Darla. I've known them for years. You'll like them, Angel," said Lenny.

I felt somewhat uncomfortable with the thought of not knowing anyone. I planned to stay close to Lenny at all times. I was unaware we would have to walk about a fourth of a mile. If I had known ahead of time, I think I would have chosen a different outfit without high heels.

By the time we arrived at the costume party and walked inside, everyone stopped dead in their tracks. Lenny and I were being stared at for what seemed like ten minutes. He said it was because I lit up the room. Zander and Darla eventually introduced themselves. Lenny had been right. I liked Zander and his wife, Darla. They were average, down-to-earth people. It was everyone else I had issues with. The party was full of snobbish, uptight people. One angel woman dressed as a cat informed me that I ruined the dessert display by taking a piece. I immediately turned to Lenny and asked if we could leave.

"I've had enough of being here. These people are rude," I said.
"Quite honestly, I agree. I'm sorry, Angel," said Lenny.
"I don't care where we go as long as we can get out of here," I informed him.
"Stand here. I'll be right back," said Lenny.

Moments later, he returned. He said Darla had a shirt, pants, and sneakers I could change into. Lenny said he had a plan. I stepped into a spare bedroom and changed into comfortable clothing. Lenny used a different room and changed into casual clothes as well. I told Darla she could keep my dress, and Lenny and I snuck out of there in an instant.

"I'm sorry, Angel. I know that was uncomfortable," he said as he led me back to the elevator.

Lenny pressed the button for Floor 19. We were headed to the floor for the season of Spring. After a short ride on the elevator, we walked out into a meadow of wildflowers.

"Run," said Lenny.
"What?" I asked.
"Run free. Come on. It will be fun," he said.

I hesitated for a moment. I then realized he was being serious. I began to run through the meadow. Lenny ran right beside me. He was absolutely right. It was so much fun. We were both smiling as we ran carefree under the Springtime sun. It was a moment to treasure.

Eventually, we ran out of breath and stopped running. I looked at Lenny and said that those people at the party were snobs.

"How is it that angels come to act like they're so much better than us? Didn't they attend Friendliness Training before entering heaven like everyone else had to?" I asked.

"Those angels have been around for centuries. They've forgotten their manners. I'm sure God has them enrolled in refresher courses," Lenny replied.

"There are refresher courses?" I asked.

"Oh, yes. For those angels who get out of line. It's not like a punishment. It's simply a reminder to them of how they are to act towards others. But let's think of something else for now," he said.

I was quite sure it was the next day by then. I had overstayed my invitation. I was only supposed to be in heaven one day. Lenny wasn't ready for me to go home, and, quite honestly, neither was I.

CHAPTER 47

Lenny and I were doing so many activities that I had no time to reflect until we found a park bench. We remained on Floor 21 in spring as we caught our breaths. After some small talk, Lenny readdressed my core insides.

"Are you going to tell me now about Ricky?" he asked.
"No. He may be alive, but he's dead to me. He's not someone I want to talk about," I adamantly replied.

Lenny finally got the message and asked no more questions.

"I think it's time we celebrate and show gratitude," Lenny said out of the blue as he changed the subject.
"What exactly do you mean?" I asked.
"It's now Sunday. God will be at his home. Let's go tell Him in person that we're grateful. Maybe we could even buy Him a gift," said Lenny.
"I can't. I'm not even supposed to be here today," I responded.
"Angel, God knows you're still here. Are you forgetting He knows everything? Come on. It will make Him happy," Lenny said.
"I'm afraid of the repercussions," I replied.

We brainstormed gift ideas for God as Lenny and I continued to sit on the park bench located by a pond. It was a difficult task to think of what to get someone who created the world. We thought He should have the best of the best. *"But what?"* we wondered as I sat staring at a toadstool. Suddenly, I had a brilliant idea – a new puppy!

"That's it! What a great idea, Angel!" Lenny nearly shouted.

Immediately we headed to the elevator and rode to Floor 70, where domesticated animals were located. Lenny warned me that there would be animals everywhere and told me to be prepared. I replied that I was ready, even though I was not expecting my next surprise.

When the elevator doors opened, Lenny and I walked into a world of animals. I had only stepped ten feet inside when, all of a sudden, a dog came running up to me. I reached down to pet her, picked her up to hold her, and began to sob.

"Awe, Angel, this is the cutest dog I have ever seen. This is a happy moment. Why the tears?" asked Lenny.
"Lenny, meet Misty. This is my childhood dog. I haven't seen her in years. These are tears of joy," I informed him.

Lenny pet Misty as I continued to hold her.

"Hello, Misty. It's nice to meet you," Lenny said as he played with Misty's ears.
"Can I help you?" said a woman's voice to us.

The woman turned out to be Nala—a woman I had originally met on the ghost train. She was a huge animal lover and worked on Floor 70, making certain the animals were well taken care of. Lenny told Nala we wanted a puppy, although he did not say it was a gift for God.

"I have just the perfect one right here. This cute fluffy white creature is a new arrival. Isn't he the most adorable thing you've ever seen?" said Nala.
"We'll take him," Lenny was quick to say.
"Wait a minute," I said as my eyes were focused on a different puppy.

As cute as the white fluffy puppy was, I was drawn to a black and gray female puppy nearby. She was busy playing with other puppies that looked to be her siblings. I could tell she had a fun-loving personality.

"I want that one," I told Nala as I pointed to the black and gray puppy.

Lenny picked up the black and gray puppy with a bright smile and began to pet her. It took no time for him to be in agreement with me. Lenny and I fell in love with the puppy instantly. The deal was done.

It was time to say goodbye to Misty, but I told her I'd be back someday. I believe she understood. We also bid farewell to Nala as Lenny and I re-entered the elevator with the new puppy.

"Where are we heading now," I asked.
"Pet grooming. Floor 37. I want everything to be perfect for God," said Lenny.

As we sat in a waiting room on Floor 37 while the puppy was being groomed, Lenny and I did some more brainstorming. We wanted to come up with a name for the new puppy. Nala had said the puppy arrived in heaven without a name.

"How about Samantha?" suggested Lenny.
"Princess Samantha," I proudly said.
"Princess Samantha, it is then. What about a middle name?" he asked.

I thought for a moment. Sitting in the waiting room brainstorming reminded me of thinking on the park bench.

"Jo! Princess Samantha Jo," I spoke with glee.

Just then, the puppy was carried out to us by the groomer. She looked so adorable that it was going to be difficult to give her away.

"Welcome back, Princess Sammy Jo," Lenny said to the puppy.

Lenny took Princess Samantha out of the arms of the groomer. He paid for the services, and we both said, "thank you." It was Sunday, so God was at his penthouse. We were off to give Him his new friendly gift.

CHAPTER 48

Lenny was so much fun to be around. I never knew where his next idea was going to lead us. I wondered where we would venture off to after visiting God. As we zoomed up the elevator to God's penthouse, Lenny told me to prepare a "thankful speech." He said he had one of his own. However, I needed to have my own personal statement. I didn't have a clue what to say. After all, I was going to be meeting face to face with The Almighty. It was nerve-wracking. My anxiety began kicking in.

"What do I say to Him?" I asked.
"What are you grateful for?" Lenny replied.
"Umm, I'm grateful to have you for a friend," I replied.
"There are numerous things to be grateful for, Angel. You need to start counting your blessings every day. You'll come up with more. It's not a hard chore," he said.

He was right. I began feeling a sense of guilt that I hadn't been counting my blessings. Before I knew it, we were there. The doors of the elevator opened, and we stood right in front of God's home. There was no time to prepare my speech. I had so much to be grateful for, yet my mind was blank.

"Go ahead. Knock on His door," instructed Lenny.

I handed Princess Sammy Jo to Lenny, stepped up on the porch, and knocked on God's door. When the door opened, God said that He had been expecting us. Although, He did seem surprised about the puppy. With a huge smile on His face, God took Princess Sammy Jo into His arms. We told Him the puppy was His to keep at His penthouse for company. God said He loved her name and that He was going to call her by the name of Sammy. It was obvious by the look on God's face that Lenny and I had done a good deed.

God invited us to step inside His home. Lenny then began his gratitude speech. I didn't hear a word he said as I was rehearsing my own speech within my head. Before I knew it, Lenny had finished and told God that I had some words to say as well. I felt unprepared, yet to my surprise, I blurted out that I was grateful to be alive. After that, I rambled on and on about the many things I thanked God for. He responded that He was pleased with me although, He instructed me to return home.

"I gave you a one-day pass for Saturday, Adalyn. This is Sunday, my dear," spoke God.

Lenny quickly stepped in and said, "That's my fault, God. I didn't want her to leave so soon. She is the best friend I have ever had. Please accept my apologies."

"Well, you did give me the cutest gift I have ever received today. Apology accepted. However, I want to be clear that this cute little puppy did not make the difference. You both knew it was wrong for Adalyn to stay an extra day. However, I understand your reasoning.

"Actually, God, I brought Adalyn here so that you could tell her to return home. I knew she wouldn't leave if I said so," said Lenny.

"Now, you're starting to sound like Matthew," I said to Lenny.

"Angel, as much as I love you as my best friend, Matthew, has been right all along. You can't stay here. We'll meet again someday, but make it a long time from now," he said.

God then instructed Lenny to lead me out of heaven. I feared going back to a lonely existence. God told me not to be afraid. He said I had all the tools I needed to make my life prosper. I thanked Him as Lenny, and I headed toward the elevator once again.

CHAPTER 49

Even though it was God who instructed me to leave heaven, I believed I would have made that choice myself. Matthew seemed happy without me, conducting the ghost train. Admittedly, my friends were all in heaven, and heaven was beyond words wonderful. Yet, God, Matthew, and Lenny were right. It wasn't my time to be there. I needed to return home. I could learn to make a meaningful life on the other side of Gray Street, where life is lived.

Lenny asked me if there was anywhere I wanted to go before leaving. I told him I would like to see the ocean one more time. We rode the elevator from God's penthouse down to Floor 78. The weather was warm and sunny. I took my shoes off and walked in the water along the beach. Lenny waited for me there. I think he knew I needed a few moments to myself.

There was a surprise for me before I actually left heaven. I don't know how the angels knew I was leaving, but they threw me a farewell party on Floor 8. I assumed God must have informed them since He was there playing drums with his band, Mr. Jones and the Noels. Matthew greeted me by handing me a bouquet of red roses. The other angels in attendance were Lenny, Alfred, Hedy, Adrielle, Carlos, Giovanni, KC, Rupert, Maurice, Nala, and Ace. I gave each one a hug and said a bittersweet goodbye.

Two hours had passed by as everyone danced to the music of the band. God motioned to Lenny that it was time. I knew that meant Lenny was to lead me out at that point. He stepped toward me and said that we had to go. Matthew took my hand as Lenny led the way. Alfred followed us as well. The four of us stepped into the elevator. I waved to God and the angels right before the door shut.

The elevator stopped on Floor 1, and the doors opened to the lobby. Standing to bid farewell were my ghostly teachers. They applauded as I stepped off the elevator. There was Mrs. Griver-Wright, her husband, Professor Wright, Mrs. Kindly, Mrs. Harper, and Mr. Robinson.

"You are a musical note. Make your life a masterpiece," Mrs. Harper advised me.

Alfred, Matthew, and I walked through the lobby and out the door to board the ghost train. Lenny followed us to the outside of the train. We said our goodbyes before I boarded.

"I will miss you with all my heart," I told Lenny.
"Goodbye, Angel. I will miss you too," he said.

We hugged without letting go of what seemed like a day. Tears were rolling down my face.

"Awe, Angel. There's no need to be sad. It's true that heaven is a better place. But you have one thing I don't. You have life. Rejoice," he simply told me.
"Yes, Sir," I said in an attempt at a little humor.

Alfred and Matthew were already on board. As I stepped onto the train, I turned back as Lenny shouted his last words to me.

"Remember to count your blessings every single day, Angel," he said.

I nodded and continued to board the train. I felt like my heart had been ripped out of my body. Matthew motioned me to take a seat. He showed no empathy for how I felt. I wondered how well I really knew Matthew. Maybe it was time to let go of him as well.

CHAPTER 50

The warmth inside the train felt more pleasing than the cool nighttime air outside. It was not difficult to find a seat as I walked down the aisle of the ghost train, still with watery eyes. The only other passenger besides myself was an old hunch-back lady wearing all black with a purple poncho. She looked alive, just as I did. I decided to sit across the aisle from her so that she wouldn't feel so lonely. Though the truth of the matter was, I thought it might help me to feel less alone. I didn't expect her to be the first to talk.

"You need to be tough in this world," she said.

I didn't know how to respond, so I simply gave her a slight nod and smile. I wondered how Lenny would have responded. He always had all of the answers and stepped in at the right moments. I thought, *"Lenny would introduce himself in this situation."* I then thought it would be polite to do just that.

"Hello. My name is Adalyn. What's your name?" I asked.
"Millie. The name's Millie. My parents named me Mildred. I go by Millie," she said with a tone of bitterness.
"It's a pleasure to meet you, Millie," I said, feeling a bit uncomfortable.

We then both sat in silence. Moments later, she spoke again.

"There arewerewolves and vampires and haunting ghosts out there," claimed Millie.
"Oh, I see," I replied with disbelief.

Nothing more was said between us. Matthew, in his role as the conductor, announced that the train was heading to Widows Peak Graveyard. The train would be picking up ghosts there before returning to Heaven's Station. He said, however, that in between those two stops, there would be a special stop on the outskirts of Flower City. I knew the special stop was for me. Millie and I continued to say nothing.

I heard the clanking sound of the train against the tracks during our silent moments. However, the rumbling didn't muffle the screeching noise coming from the ghost train. It was a sound I had never heard before. I wasn't certain if it was just my imagination or whether the train had a slight wobble.

All of a sudden, the ghost train lights went dead. My heart began to race in panic.

"This is my stop," Millie informed me.
"But there's nothing out there," I replied with concern.

Millie grabbed her cane, stood up, and pointed out my window.

"See that old cabin up ahead? That's my home," she said.

As I focused my eyes see into the distance, I viewed nothing but darkness. The doors opened as Millie walked up the aisle and exited the train. *"I thought that Matthew said the only stop besides the graveyard and Heaven's Station was the outskirts of Flower City,"* I said to myself. I approached Matthew for clarification.

"Why did we make a stop here?" I asked.
"This was an emergency stop. The train has been having a bit of trouble, but it's nothing to worry yourself about. Alfred's outside inspecting the train as we speak," Matthew replied.
"But that old woman. She left the train," I exclaimed.
"It's okay, Adalyn. She wasn't supposed to be riding the train anyway. She's a witch," he informed me.

I was spooked! *"The old woman was a witch?"* I repeated inside my head to engrain an understanding. Just then, Alfred stepped on board to inform Matthew that the train appeared to be fine. He returned to his seat to engineer the train. The ghost train was back in operation, rolling down the tracks, yet still with a tad bit of a screech.

CHAPTER 51

Matthew and I engaged in small talk before reaching Widows Peak Graveyard. There were twenty-six new ghost arrivals. It was the most crowded I had ever seen the train. I later asked Matthew why there were so many ghosts at this one particular stop. He explained that it was the hub of graveyards. He told me to think of it as though it was the main bus stop.

I was so glad that no one sat down next to me. Lenny had always had that spot, and there wasn't anyone who could take his place. Matthew spoke into the microphone as it was routine to instruct new ghosts about their ride. As planned, he said there would be a stop near Flower City before arrival at Heaven's Station. Therefore, I would be the only one to exit at the next stop.

The train jolted suddenly. I thought it was about to come to a complete halt, but it continued down the tracks. I hoped that Alfred would fully inspect the train's maintenance once it arrived at Heaven's Station. In the meantime, I held onto faith that the train would bring me safely to my stop.

I talked to none of the other passengers. However, I overheard two ghosts commenting on my appearance. They said that I looked rather odd to be a ghost. I was not about to waste my breath, explaining to them that I was alive. I wasn't positive, but I thought I heard one of the ghosts exclaim that I was possibly a witch. I certainly was not a witch. In fact, I didn't know witches even truly existed until I met Millie.

I thought the train was never going to reach the outskirts of Flower City. The crowded train was beginning to annoy me. I had no desire to meet anyone or start a conversation. The ghosts were nothing like the ones I originally met on the train. They were all merely strangers to me.

After an hour of wallowing in thought, the train stopped, and the door flew open. I had finally reached the first destination of my trip back home. Maybe saying goodbye to Matthew was in the back of my mind, but I realized it hadn't been at the forefront. This was it. The moment of truly saying goodbye to him had arrived.

"It seems we've been through these goodbyes before," said Matthew.
"I know. I won't be back again until God says it's my time," I replied.
"That's good to hear. By the way, honey, I have some good news to share," he added.

I was surprised to hear Matthew address me as "honey." He hadn't called me that in months. He then went on to tell me his news.

"I am being promoted," he said.
"Congratulations. What's the next step beyond being the conductor?" I asked.
"An international flight pilot. I have always had an interest in trains and aviation—actually, anything that travels," he went on to inform me.
"So, you have your pilot license?" I questioned.
"Yes, of course. I had taken lessons during the course of my life. I completed the course in heaven. I will be flying around the world on the ghost plane, picking up ghosts from everywhere and bringing them to heaven," said Matthew.
"I see that you are truly happy where you are," I said with a confident smile.
"I really am, Adalyn. I'm sorry we didn't have much time together during your stay in heaven. God works in mysterious ways. Maybe I was sent to heaven for a good reason. So that I could fulfill my dreams, it might not have worked out for us, honey. Just do one thing that I ask of you, okay?" he said.
"Okay. What is it?" I asked.

"Just remember me. That's all," he said.

I felt my eyes begin to swell, and a tear fell down my face. Matthew wiped the tear off, smiled, and said his goodbyes. God knew that I needed to move on with my life, and He knew that Matthew needed to be of great purpose in heaven. Maybe I had been led to heaven to discover just that. I stepped off the train and crossed Gray Street back into the world of the living.

CHAPTER 52

Upon entering the crowded Flower City Express train station, I heard my name being called. The woman shouting, who appeared to be in her forties, was approaching me.

"Adalyn! It's so wonderful to see you after all of these years," said the unrecognizable woman.
"I'm sorry, but do I know you?" I asked her.
"Adalyn. It's me! Wendy Avalara. Well, my married name is now Wendy Jamison, but you knew me when I was Wendy Avalara," she said.

I couldn't believe my eyes. Wendy had been my closest friend in high school. We hadn't seen each other in decades. The years had blessed her well as she had aged gracefully. Wendy had been a "Plain Jane" in our school days.

"Oh, yes, Wendy! It's been so long," I said.
"The train is about to leave. Are you taking the Express into Flower City?" she asked.
"Yes. I need to purchase my ticket," I informed her.
"Go ahead. Hurry up. I'll wait for you here, and we can find a seat together," said Wendy.

The train was not as crowded as the station. After purchasing my ticket with money that Matthew gave me, Wendy and I found seats next to one another. It was a short ride into Flower City, so we didn't have a lot of time to reacquaint. We briefly summed up our lives.

"What have you been up to all of these years?" asked Wendy.

"Well, I worked at Powers Corporation. Then I took some time off. I did the routine daily chores and dated here and there," I said, knowing I hadn't lived an exciting life.

"Oh, I see. How about vacations? Have you traveled any?" she asked.

"Some train trips, but never out of the country," I replied.

"Oh, that's nice," Wendy said, trying to smile genuinely.

"How about you? What have you been up to?" I reciprocated.

"I'm married with two children. Two boys. No grandbabies yet. My husband, Donald, made certain our finances were in gear so that I could stay at home to raise the kids. My boy, William, opened his own business, so now I work for him. He treats me well. He has to. I'm his mother," she said with laughter.

Wendy's life seemed to have taken an envious path. Yet, I was not about to indulge in self-pity. Lenny"s last words to me were to count my blessings. As well, I needed to reverse my way of thinking and revel in the blessings of others.

"I'm so happy for you. I know it's a bit late, but congratulations on having your children. I never had any of my own, but my late boyfriend, Matthew, had two grown daughters," I said in an attempt to fill the void of being childless.

"You said your late boyfriend? I'm sorry. He has passed away?" Wendy asked for clarification.

"Yes, he passed away earlier this year. I've spent the remaining months in mourning. I'm at a point now where I am ready to plan a life without him," I said.

"May he rest in peace," Wendy said with sympathy.

I nodded, even though my insides were filled with laughter. There was no resting in peace for Matthew. He had other plans. He was about to pilot a plane all over the world! However, I told Wendy thank you and hoped my face wasn't displaying even the slightest smile.

"Again, I'm so sorry for your loss," Wendy said.

"Thank you," I replied.

She paused momentarily and then asked, "Do you mind if I change the subject?"

"No, not at all," I replied.

"Okay. Well, do you remember when we bumped into each other that one time at the grocery store?" Wendy asked.

"Yes, how could I forget? You weren't married at the time, and the man in the frozen foods department was flirting up a storm with you," I said as we both burst out in laughter.

"Wow, I had forgotten that part. And you were with Ricky. He was so handsome. What ever happened to him?" she curiously asked.

"We parted ways. I haven't seen him in years. But you're a married woman. You can't have him," I said as we both laughed once again.

"I know. But he did seem perfect for you," she added.

I felt an ache inside my stomach, just talking about Ricky. However, I was "saved by the bell" when the train whistle sounded. We had reached our Flower City destination. I had so many laughs with Wendy that I hardly wanted to say goodbye. Suddenly, I recalled inviting Sabrina and River Wilson to a get-together. I then invited Wendy as well.

"I'm having a small party at my house soon to reacquaint with old friends. I would be delighted to have you there," I said right before we went our separate ways.

"Of course! Here's my phone number. Just call and let me know when and where," said Wendy as she handed me her number.

Wendy had a ride waiting for her at the station. I hailed a taxi back home. I would soon be preparing invitations for old friends.

CHAPTER 53

The taxi made a right turn into Hedy's Way neighborhood. There were only a few side streets to pass before reaching my home on Adalyn Drive. I told the taxi driver to simply follow the signs leading to the Leonard Calvin Deter Memorial Park. I thought I would stop there first before walking a short distance to my house. The taxi pulled into the parking lot. I paid for the ride and stepped out. Not a soul was around. I sat on the same park bench I had before when I had encountered Lenny. It was a good thing the park was vacant, or else people would have seen me talking to myself.

"Well, Lenny. This is it. God gave me the wings to fly, and you showed me how. I'm ready to finally live a full and meaningful life. One, two, three, four. Hey, Lenny. I'm counting my blessings," I said in an attempt to be funny and grab his attention.

I thought by talking out loud to Lenny, he might appear. Though, the only sound in the park that day was my voice and the wind whispering through the trees. Even the birds were unusually silent.

I could see that I was not going to be able to manipulate a lonely situation. I believed Lenny was gone from me for good. I still had God to talk and pray to, however. There was only one task left for me to do. I needed to stop talking about living life and begin to live it. I stood up and walked home.

My house was dark inside upon entering the front door. The shades were drawn, lights were off, and Matthew was not there to greet me as he once had been. I turned the living room light switch on and peered at my lifeless home. *"Count your blessings. You have a home. You're alive and well. You have friends. This is not the time to be mourning,"* I thought to myself.

It actually worked! I thought of all the things I am grateful for, and I began to feel better. On my way to the kitchen to get a bite to eat, I noticed something shiny coming from my darkened bedroom. I walked toward my nightstand and picked the shiny object up from the floor. It was my necklace with a locket and the key to life. I suddenly felt ashamed of myself for accusing Matthew's daughter of taking it. I had it all along.

After a few days of resettling in, it was time to plan for my small get-together with old friends. I first made out my list of the people I was going to invite. From school days, I would invite Wendy, Maria, Alicia, and Morgan. I added to the list my former co-workers, Sidney, Jonathan, Roberta, Sabrina, and her daughter, River. Since I had no idea how to contact anyone but Wendy and Sabrina, I asked them both if they knew their phone numbers. As luck would have it, Wendy had kept in touch with the other school friends, and Sabrina had stayed in contact with the remaining co-workers. Unfortunately, not everyone was able to attend. Morgan and Roberta had pre-existing plans. However, I did spend time on the phone talking to both of them separately. We caught up about our lives with one another. We then made plans to get together after the holidays.

Since it was nearly time for the winter holidays, I wanted to decorate my house for the season. I asked my next-door neighbor if he could help put up lights outside my house. He was helpful in doing so. His wife directed us on the correct placement of the lights as we both stood on ladders. It felt good to be connecting with living human beings.

The outside lights were up, and my house inside was decorated for the holidays. I had invited each friend and their spouse via a phone call. Every single one of them was surprised to hear from me. I apologized for my disappearance from their lives. I had no excuse other than my own depression. Though, that was in the past. I was determined to rearrange my life and rekindle old friendships. The party was set to begin.

CHAPTER 54

My guests had all arrived. Wendy showed up with her husband, Donald. The two made a lovely couple. As well, Jonathan and his wife, Stephanie, and Maria and her boyfriend, Jerry, seemed as though they were made for one another. Alicia and Sidney were by themselves, and Sabrina had her daughter, River, with her. Including me, there were eleven people at my house.

After introducing my co-worker friends and their guests to my school friends and their guests, we reminisced with nothing but laughter. My friends' guests even found interest and humor in the stories being told. I smiled so much my face hurt, and my stomach got a workout from all the laughing I did. It made me wonder to myself why I had ever disconnected and lost touch with my friends. I had momentarily left the remembrance of my past depression behind.

Wendy stepped me aside to tell me there was one person I had forgotten to invite. She said she had extended an invitation to my party. Wendy then apologized for overstepping her boundaries. As I was about to tell her not to be concerned, the doorbell rang. I opened the door and, to my surprise, there he was! Ricky was standing at my doorstep. As I gazed into his warm brown eyes, heartache instantly disappeared. He was as though I was staring at my future.

THE END

REFERENCE

Ghosts to Angels Graduate Ceremony Brochure

Welcome to Heaven. The graduation ceremony is held on Saturday is a celebration of ghosts becoming angels. God is here to welcome and congratulate each graduate. After the ceremony, please enjoy the music of God's band, "Mr. Jones and the Noels." Dancing is encouraged.

Below is a list of the floors of Heaven to aid in your travel and leisure choices. In the event there is somewhere missing that you would prefer was included, a suggestion box can be found at the entrance to God's Prayer Offices on Floor 11. Please enjoy your stay!

Elevator Floors

0B	Basement - Student Room & Board
01	Reservations
02	Forgiveness Training
03	Friendliness Training
04	Music Class
05	Giving Training
06	Love Training
07	Heaven's Gate
08	Concerts
09	Mailroom
10	Wishes Offices
11	God's Prayer Offices
12	Hall of Fame

13	Bugs
14	Dancing
15	Sports
16	Race Car Driving
17	Stargazing
18	Shopping Mall with Trolleys
19	Spring
20	Summer
21	Autumn
22	Winter
23	Rain
24	Restaurants
25	Movie Theaters
26	Playgrounds/Parks
27	Technology
28	Art Museums
29	Music Studios
30	Plays
31	Entrance to Lookout Tower
32	Neighborhoods
33	Libraries
35	Movie Studios
36	Art
37	Pet Grooming
38	Real Estate Office
39	Bank
40-69	More Neighborhoods
70	Domestic Animals
71	Wild Animal Jungle
72	Camping
73	Television Studios
74	Radio Studios
75	Fashion Design Workshops
76	Casinos
77	Card and Board Games
78	Beaches

79	Boating/Fishing/Water Sports
80	Sea Life Heaven
81	Prehistoric Creatures' Heaven
82	Dress Up Studios
83	Cooking
84	Parallel Universes
85	Gardens and Waterfalls
86	Hiking
87	Aviation
88	Worship and Retreats
89	Cities
90	Countrysides
91	Ski Slopes
92	Amusement Parks
93	Water Parks
94	Video Games
95	World of Make Believe
96	Chit Chat Rooms
97	Musical Instrument Studies
98-451	All Other Schools and Training Centers
452	Aliens' Heaven
453	Meditation and Yoga
454	Hair Salons/Spas/Barber Shops
455-776	More Neighborhoods
777	Club 777
778-848	More Neighborhoods
849	Rebirth Application Offices
850-998	More Neighborhoods
999-2	Below Infinity A Floor for Every Year
1 Below Infinity	God's Penthouse

Giovanni's Corner Restaurant Vegetarian Dinner Menu

Halo and Welcome

Appetizers

Wings
Salvation Fried Cauliflower

Main Dishes

St. Anthony's Spaghetti & Meatballs
Almighty Cheeseburger
Paradise Surprise
Pearly Gates Tuna Sandwich

Side Dishes

Blissful French Fries
Blessed Coleslaw
Eternal Mixed Salad

Desserts

Cloud 9 Ice Cream (1,000 Flavors)
Angel Food Cake
Sky High Pie
Sinfully Delicious Brownie
Holy Doughnut

Beverages

Water
Wine

www.ingramcontent.com/pod-product-compliance
Lightning Source LLC
LaVergne TN
LVHW040150080526
838202LV00042B/3099